THE HARRISONS

RICHARD M BELOIN MD

authorHOUSE®

AuthorHouse™
1663 Liberty Drive
Bloomington, IN 47403
www.authorhouse.com
Phone: 1 (800) 839-8640

Published by AuthorHouse 05/19/2020

ISBN: 978-1-7283-6153-6 (sc)
ISBN: 978-1-7283-6170-3 (e)

Print information available on the last page.

This book is printed on acid-free paper.

CONTENTS

DEDICATION

I dedicate this book to my son, David. He was the first and persistent with the idea that I should write my first sequel.

PREFACE

This western fiction is a sequel to "Jake Harrison—US Marshal. Although it can be an independent self-standing fiction, the basic content of the first in this series is well presented in this book's Prologue.

If you wish to know the details of the interpersonal relationship that has led to this sequel, I recommend you take the time and read the original story as it was always intended to be presented.

PROLOGUE

'HOW WE GOT HERE'

Jake was a native Texan, born in Waco, the son of Amos and Erna Harrison. Amos was the local sheriff and Erna was a dressmaker. At an early age of fourteen, Jake went to work part-time in a gun shop. By his 10th grade graduation, Jake had learned to perform firearm action jobs and repairs. Until his 18th birthday, he worked full time in the gun shop.

During these two years, Jake learned the mastery of firearms. He became a fast draw expert with a Colt Peacemaker and a short-range rifle marksman with the Win 73. Eventually, he mastered long-range shooting up to 400 yards with a scoped Win 76 in 45-70.

At age 18, Jake went to work for his father as a deputy sheriff. Under Amos' tutelage, he learned the local and county laws as well as how to make safe arrests and many tricks of the trade. After one year on the job, Jake became disillusioned with the jurisdiction restrictions which allowed outlaws to escape out of the community once beyond 25 miles out of town. So, he resigned his lawman status and became a bounty hunter pending his entrance in the Lawman School—a preparatory and almost a prerequisite to the US Marshal Service.

His months as a solo bounty hunter proved to be a dangerous profession although productive with experience and bounty rewards. During these months he participated in man hunts, saloon and outlaw camp arrests, murder investigations, terminating train robberies, protecting stagecoaches, and outright gun fights—man to man.

During this bounty hunting period, Jake amassed a large bank account. It was at this time that he realized victims of violent crimes could be helped financially by his bank holdings. This financial support of victims became the introduction to Jake's Benefactor Fund.

His four months in the Denver Lawman School was a learning experience. He had classes in Colorado/Texas law, theory and practice of safe arrests, self-defense in hand-to-hand combat, and firearms training. His prowess with firearms eventually led to his becoming the firearm instructor's assistant. Other than the training, Jake met and became best of friends with Willie—who later became his deputy.

Entering in the US Marshal Service, Jake was placed in a four-man confrontational squad. During the year, his squad appreciated Jake's knowledge of jungle warfare and use of tools of the trade. His fast draw skill in a gunfight saved his squad several times. When the squad leader retired, he was voted the new squad sergeant and leader.

After the sudden death of Jake's sister and brother-in-law, he was sent to New Braunfels to root out his family's killers. This was the beginning of Jake's future. Here he met his future bride and reconnected with his old friend, Willie Irving.

***

Jake met Hannah accidentally and only to find three men about to sexually assault her. After rescuing her, he felt an attraction that lead to supporting her emotionally and financially. Things just naturally progressed to love, cohabitating and marriage.

Hannah was known as the 'egg lady' in town. Jake built up her laying hen brood with enough producers to make the enterprise profitable. Hannah went from 50 layers to 400 laying hens separated in two massive coops and runs. Hannah presented every detail regarding chicken's maintenance and egg production to Jake, who became a willing participant in the chicken/egg business.

Hannah had a secret love which was revealed by her talking in her sleep. Being the daughter of a Literature professor, she had been an avid reader and actually became secondarily self-educated beyond the 10th grade. Her secret love was the wish to write her own novel. When realizing this, Jake provided her with the equipment to type her book and arranged to send her to the local community college for a course in grammar, composition, and speed typing.

Meanwhile, Jake also became involved in cattle ranching and crop farming. Having inherited his sister's ranch, Jake became interested in changing his herd of Texas Longhorns to crossbreeds. Finding a source of polled Hereford and Durham Short Horn bulls, the herd's genetic makeup was changed to the more productive crossbred animal.

Crop farming provided a new venture for Jake. Learning the process of cultivating, fertilizing, seeding, harvesting and baling hay and straw was a new potential for profit. Along the way, the storage buildings and extra implements provided a method of achieving this enterprise. With the expansion of more cultivated lands, the business grew exponentially and became a separate division from cattle ranching.

***

Amidst all this activity, Jake was hunting for his family's killers. Tied in with the suspected killers was a crooked sheriff and prosecuting attorney. After arresting both these men for malfeasance and obstruction of justice, Jake found a prosecutor in the Denver Marshal Service who ended up sending these two to prison.

After a gunfight with the killer's gunslingers, Jake was able to get a death bed statement implicating the killer and his son. This, along with another of the killer's gunfighters turning state's evidence, the local judge issued an arrest warrant. Jake and Willie proceeded to the killer's ranch to make the arrest of Hans and Kurt Klaus.

When Jake informed the senior Klaus that they were both under arrest for murder and ordering the unlawful killing of settlers, the son knew he was going to hang, so he went for his gun. Willie responded and shot him dead with a shotgun blast.

The senior Klaus was tried for ordering multiple murders in his attempt to get hold of more land with surface oil. After the judge selected a jury, he missed a biased juror. Somehow, Klaus was able to buy a juror which led to a mistrial. The Marshal Service prosecutor convinced the judge to retry the case immediately. This time the lawyers would choose the jury with the right to refuse any potential juror who may be in financial difficulties and a likely target for the defense. The trial ended in a unanimous guilty verdict and Hans Klaus was hung.

***

The Harrisons were looking at the future. With the arrival of Hans Klaus' estranged adopted son, uncertainty existed. The duo also looked ahead in commercializing the egg business, adding meat birds, growing the crop business to all the local ranchers and beyond, offering crossbred and purebred bulls to ranchers, digging for oil, writing a novel, and establishing a Marshal Service locally.

The head of the Marshal Service in Denver had offered Jake the southern district leadership under the newly named judgeship of Harland Hobart. If Jake was to accept the position, he would need to recruit two more deputies, other than Willie, and establish an office and jail in New Braunfels.

AND SO, LIFE IN SOUTH TEXAS' 1900'S, CONTINUES

***

CHAPTER 1

RECRUITING US MARSHALS

Life in New Braunfels had become a pleasurable contentment. Hannah was spending her mornings caring for the 250 laying hens in the chicken coop located next to the ranch's barn. She would water and feed the brood at daylight and hours later, after her own breakfast, would release them to the run with ample seeds to scratch and peck. After the chickens were released, she would pack the eggs and deliver, every other day, a six-dozen flat to the three mercantiles, Fischer, Lehmann and Wolfgang.

Leaving the ranch with her three egg flats totaling 18 dozen, Jake would smile seeing his lovely wife riding the new buggy with the dangling sign below the tailgate that read, 'egg lady.' What Jake mostly appreciated was the loaded double barrel shotgun anchored to the seat's scabbard as well as her loaded 44 Webley Bulldog in her belted holster.

Hannah had become a speed crack shot with her pistol. She could place a bullet in five man-size targets at ten feet in less than five seconds because of the speed of a double action pistol. Every evening after supper, the duo went to their private range and practiced shooting.

Although the bulk of Hannah's time was spent on the pistol, Hannah also practiced shooting the shotgun, especially speed reloading by shucking shells backwards and adding two new shells to the chambers simultaneously. Jake had impressed on her to always wear her Bulldog. Hannah's eyebrows went up when Jake said, "it's better to have a gun and not need it, than to need a gun and not have it." In addition, Jake emphasized that a gun in a drawer or in another room is not a gun that can be used in self-defense. The final impressive comment from Jake was, "until we know how things will work out with Dieter Klaus, we need to be ready at all times. And that means, wearing your pistol in the house, heh!"

The other going-on was Jake's parents living with the newlyweds while their house, windmill well, indoor plumbing and barn were being built by Cass Construction's foreman, Elliot Billings and crew. While Hannah was delivering eggs, Amos' duty was to walk the chicken run's perimeter looking for coyotes who were waiting nearby. Loaded with #3 Buck, with its twenty ¼ inch lead pellets, they created havoc with the predators and the daily hunt kept their numbers at bay.

It being fall, the newly cultivated 100 acres of oats were ready for harvest. Jake had the time and decided to watch the entire process. To his surprise, no mower was used. Instead the oats were cut with a machine called a binder. This cut the oats, made a bunch called shocks, which were tied with a string, and loaded on a shadowing flatbed wagon. Thereafter, the shocks were brought to the thresher where the seeds were knocked off the stalks. The remainder of the light chaff was then removed with the winnower. Left over was straw and oats seeds (grain).

The only other local activity was Hannah's writing and typing progress. Initially, she had trouble typing the letters using the pinky and ring finger of each hand, but worse on her weaker left hand. The college instructor had given her two 2-inch rubber balls to use three times a day to exercise and strengthen her fingers. It had worked and Hannah passed the typing part of her course when she typed 50 correct words per minute. Hannah pointed out that typing at 1½ spacing yielded +-250 words per page, or 7-8 minutes per page—typing slower to avoid typos.

The composition part was finished, and Hannah passed a completion exam. She then registered for the next course given in writing. This course's goal was to get each student to start writing a fiction under supervision—and Hannah was ready to start. Hannah had designated 1—5PM daily to writing, studying and maintaining typing skills. To have this time to herself, her house cleaning, laundry, cooking was all done after the chicken duties and deliveries. Wednesday afternoons were spent at the college from 3—5PM for her writing course. During the class time, Jake ran errands. After class, they went to Bessie's Diner for supper and were generally back home by dark.

***

The perpetually delayed meeting with the head of the US Marshal Service was finally scheduled. In anticipation, Jake decided to interview the one cowhand who could work out as a deputy US Marshal. Jake met with the Apache, Rocky, who was in charge of the barn and remuda along with his Indian wife, Red Flower.

Meeting in his office, Jake started. "What brings you here to work when you can have all your needs met in the reservation."

"Several reasons. There is nothing to do in the reservation. My people are slowly starving and need clothing. The government handouts are not enough. So, because I like to be active, I work here and give most of my wages to my family in the reservation. Besides, Red Flower likes the work, the cowboys and the cropboys, as much as I do."

"What is your and Red Flower's pay"

"You pay us $55 per month and all but $10 goes to our people in the reservation"

"Ok, let me explain why I asked to speak to you. I'm organizing a US Marshal squad and I need a tracker. Clayton tells me you can do the job. Are you interested?"

"Certainly, I would include it as one of my duties."

"No this would be extra. As a temporary deputy, you would be paid $10 per day and would share in the bounty rewards with the remainder of the squad. Clayton also told me you were an expert rifle shooter. Can you shoot and kill a white man who is trying to kill you?"

"I'll take the job and will do what is necessary, that includes shooting an outlaw, of any race or culture."

"Can you work with a black man; Willie will be on the squad?"

"Of course."

"Leaving the barn at a moment's notice, can Red Flower take over the barn duties till you return."

"Yes, without a doubt."

"Then we have a deal. Welcome to the squad. Raise your right hand and repeat after me. Now here is your badge that you only wear when on assignments. We'll have our first meeting with you and Willie once I add two more members."

***

The next day Jake and Hannah rode to introduce themselves to their new neighbor, Dieter Klaus. Hannah reminded Jake to keep control of the meeting and only accept a business deal if it was to their benefit. Arriving at the ranch it was clear that the cattle had been replaced by oil drilling equipment. After entering the ranch house, they were escorted to Dieter's office by his secretary/accountant.

Entering the office, Dieter stood and came

to shake Hannah's hand as he said, "welcome Hannah, I remember you from our school days, but you have certainly blossomed into a lovely lady. Now you sir, I know you are a US Marshal, but you killed my brother and had my estranged father hung. That will never change, but I'm willing to put that aside for now. So, what brings you here today?"

Jake took over, "We have a business proposition for you. We know that you are trying to lease the several homesteads that your family acquired. We are told that this includes the house, barn and a 5-acre lot for a coral, pasture and garden but excludes oil or mineral rights."

"Yes, that is correct. If you're interested, make me an offer and we'll see how close you are to my leasing price and conditions."

Realizing that the man was setting condescending rules of engagement that needed to be met, Jake continued. "We would like to lease the two homesteads east of my ranch. We would offer you, per homestead, $100 per year and pay the property taxes on the buildings and

5 acres. We would fence in the acreage, maintain the buildings, and pay for any improvements we chose to add. For this consideration, we would like a fixed leasing cost for the next 10 years."

"Instead of leasing, if you're willing to give me the oil and mineral rights to the Bauer section of 640 acres, I will trade you the two homestead houses, barns and the five acres."

"That is not possible. The Bauer deed has been changed to me and Hannah and the land or mineral rights are not for sale. In addition, my ranch to include three sections is not for sale and the mineral rights are also not for sale. I'm seriously thinking of digging an oil test well."

"Well in that case, there is not enough instant money to be talking of leases. My oil drilling plans need operating cash. So, I will sell the two homesteads along with a total of 20 acres for $2,000."

"That's an interesting option although a bit expensive. Let me counteroffer, sell us four of the homesteads east of us with house, barn and 10 acres each for a total of $3,700. If you accept, I will give you a deposit of 10% today, and we'll meet at the town clerk's office tomorrow with the final payment and we'll sign the deed. You'll have to pay back-taxes if there are any."

Dieter paused and was doing some computations. He then whispered to his accountant and waited for his response. After a fairly long wait, the Harrisons began to think that the offer was about to be rejected. Suddenly Dieter said, "I will do this deal as long as a restrictive covenant is agreed to."

"Which states what?"

"That you or the any of the next owners cannot place an oil well on the 10 acres for a minimum of 7 years from today."

"Can Hannah and I have a moment to discuss this?"

"Certainly."

Hannah starts, *"the price is still a bit high, but when we realize why we want these homes, it really isn't. We're buying four homesteads as private homes for our ranch workers or for some of the deputy marshals. The oil restrictive covenant is not really important or relevant. I say we take the deal."*

Jake looks up at Dieter and says, "Deal." A

bill of sale was prepared by the accountant and signed by all four participants. Jake included a bank draft of $370 and all agreed to meet in town tomorrow morning before Jake and Hannah took the train to Denver.

***

The Harrisons picked up their free tickets, courtesy of Mr. Duseldorf. Because of the long train ride to cover 900 miles, they paid for Pullman berths and for all meals in the dining car. Hannah had her textbook on writing and one on advanced composition. Jake was reading a current publication on the recent advancement in firearms and a second book on drilling for oil. For entertainment, Hannah had a 400- page novel on a family moving along the Oregon Trail and settling in Washington's Willamette Valley. This publication was suggested by the college instructor as a writing in the style Hannah wanted to emulate.

As the train moved along, liquid refreshments and snacks were served in the dining car in mid-morning and mid-afternoon. The three full meals were well attended by the paying passengers. As the miles added on, Jake went over with Hannah the new firearms available in the 1900's.

"The double barrel shotgun is now available in a hammerless version with a tang fire/safe safety. This is an advantage in reloading since a manual re-cock is not necessary. I plan to give each man a sawed-off shotgun with backpack holster, and a longer barrel coach gun—both hammerless. In addition, I will change the caliber from 12 gauge to 10 gauge. This increases the total number of .33-inch pellets from 9 to 12 per shell. Plus, these new shotguns will have stronger steel barrels to handle smokeless powder. This will start negating the powder bloom of black powder which gives away the location of the shooter or obscures their vision in a close-up gunfight. In case of a shortage in 10-gauge shells, a chamber sleeve can be added to the 10-gauge gun to temporarily use 12-gauge shells in an emergency."

"In 1900, we now have the choice of moving up to a pump shotgun from the old standby double barrel shotgun. This pump 1897 Model is a slide action shotgun with a hammer that is only available in 12-gauge. It has the higher carbon steel to handle smokeless powder shells. It is a fast repeater that holds 1 shell in the chamber and 5 in the tubular magazine. I suspect that this pump will replace the double in a short time."

Hannah added, "so, what type are you offering your men." "Wyllie has already bought an 1897 pump and loves it. He's only keeping his sawed-off shotgun if he's walking about town or as a backup firearm."

"Hannah added, "would you get me one, I'd like to get use to a pump instead of the heavier double barrel type."

"Of course. Now, Rocky is a different matter. As an Apache Indian, he wears a knife and uses a Winchester 73 rifle. For everyday use, he is not comfortable with a single action Colt Peacemaker. So, I've given him a new Colt Model 1898. This is a 45 Long Colt in a double action revolver. He wears this in a cross-draw holster that is comfortable riding a horse.

He's been practicing and is doing very well not having to cock the hammer. I actually think he's enjoying this pistol."

"The new thing in rifles is the Winchester 1894 lever action. It is made of hardened steel that handles smokeless powder. It fires a 30 caliber bullet at a minimum of 1800 fps. Because of the longer cartridge, the tubular feed only handles five or six rounds depending on the length of the tubular feed, plus one round in the chamber. Unlike the 44-40 caliber, this 30-30 is easily a 100-200-yard gun. Otherwise, for long range shooting, +-350 yards, we'll stay with the scoped Win 76 in 45-70 caliber and hope that they come out with a smokeless round in this caliber."

Hannah asks, "is there anything new in mini pistols to replace my 44 caliber DA Bulldog?"

"There are many mini pistols coming out, especially in Colt. Yet, these are all in 38 caliber. I don't see any improvements worthwhile replacing our Bulldog until they come out with a mini six shot 41 or 44 caliber."

Arriving in Amarillo, trains were changed,

and their passenger and Pullman berths were added to the northbound train to Colorado. Replenishing the dining car, the train was off for its second leg.

Sleeping in the Pullman berths was easy. The wheels clanging on the track joints with the gentle side to side rocking was conducive to falling and maintaining sleep. Having a deluxe berth had its own privy.

It took some time to get comfortable seeing the tracks, at the bottom of the pit, moving along at 30 mph. The droppings would splatter on the tracks and disappear. It was Hannah who commented, "now I know why my mom always told me not to walk on the rails or railroad ties."

After traveling some 30 hours, the duo arrived in Denver at 11AM. Getting a quick dinner at a diner close to the marshal headquarters, they arrived at Captain Ennis' office on time. The first person they came into contact with was Deputy Marshal Clifton Gibson, esquire.

Jake shook Clifton's hand and said, "thanks again for prosecuting the crooked sheriff, prosecutor and Hans Klaus. I owe you a favor and I always pay my debts. What is new for you?"

"Well, your federal judge, Harland Hobart, and your district judge, Hoyt Aiken, are both looking for a joint prosecutor and not having luck finding one. I volunteered for the job, but the Captain is not warming up to the idea. My wife is not happy in the big city and wants to get back to Texas since she's from Austin."

Hannah asked, "how did she ever end up in Denver to meet you?"

"Well, she came to a school here to study olericulture and became friends with another student from Dallas. This friend, Sylvia Adams, ironically returned to Texas and established a vegetable growing and canning empire in Alamo, whereas my wife from Austin met me and stayed in Denver for the past five years. Now, it's only a matter of time before we end up in South Texas for the warm weather. My wife has not adjusted to the Colorado winters."

Jake was listening to all this and could see several potentials. "Say Clifton, we'll be spending the night at the Claymore Hotel.

Why don't you and your wife join us for supper at the hotel's Ruby Restaurant followed by a comedy play at the Hill Theater?"

"Those are words to my wife's ears. Certainly, how about at 5PM since the theater opens at 8PM. We'll meet you in the hotel lobby."

Entering the Captain's office, Captain Ennis came up to shake Hannah and Jake's hands. "Welcome to the big city, that was a long 30- hour trip to get here, so I appreciate you both making the trip. Shall we get down to business?"

"I'm pleased that you have accepted the position of heading the Southern District. Now the issue is whether you can leave your enterprises to do this job."

"Yes, I believe we've covered the bases. My father is now living next door and will protect Hannah, besides she can now take care of herself. My ranch and crop manager can handle the business without me. The egg enterprise is controlled by Hannah and several employees. If I decide to dig for oil, it will be managed with appropriate workmen."

"Are you planning to work the Marshal Service on a daily basis versus on a 'as needed basis.'"

"My three deputies will handle the day to day processes, court duties and prisoner transfers. I will get involved in manhunts, range wars, mining uprisings, gold and silver transfers, judicial protection, and other special events."

"That is perfect. You are delegating duties, yet get involved in serious and dangerous capers. Now, how much help do you want?"

"I already have a deputy, Willie Irving. I also will use my Indian wrangler as tracker on an 'as needed basis," and will pay him $10 per day and his share of bounty rewards. I'm looking for an experienced US Marshal and a newbie out of Lawman School."

"Ironically, I have both of these men available. Let's start with the experienced marshal. It is your old partner, Furman Belcher. He has three boys ages 14,16 and 18. They have been working crops part-time for local homesteaders, and are looking for more permanent work. In addition, Furman needs a change and is happy to be working with you. The real push is Furman's wife, Laura. She has never adjusted being a German/Lutheran in a big city and looks forward to moving to a German community like New Braunfels with a Lutheran church and pastor. In addition, as she ages, she is getting leery of her husband being a lawman and sees an advantage for Furman to be working for you, heh. FYI, Furman has become an expert pump shotgun shooter using the Win 1897 pump. He also has a cut down version with a pistol grip in a backpack holster like you developed. After our meeting, Furman and Laura will be here for you to interview them."

"Great, what about this newbie out of Lawman School?"

"His name is Walt Garnett age 22. He is single and also ironically, is from Dallas Texas. He has expressed a strong wish to return to Texas. His past experience was being a bounty hunter with a partner. When his partner got killed, he then joined the Lawman School. His expertise is with firearms. He's like you, a fast draw expert. I strongly recommend him, but you also need to meet with him today after the Belchers."

"Now the finances. Each marshal will receive, from the Colorado Marshal Service, a salary of $100 per month with disability and medical benefits. These funds are subsidized by the Texas government. Judge Hobart has a budget which includes his salary. Any bounty rewards are yours to distribute as you wish with your deputies. Petty cash from outlaw pockets and saddlebags are yours to share. Any confiscated horses and firearms are to be sold and the value deposited in the Colorado US Marshal Service. Any confiscated cash is to be returned to victims if possible. Any amount left over will be divided equally between three entities—The US Marshal Service, Judge Hobart's account, and you. What you do with your share is your business."

"Well, this is more than I expected. So, what is the catch?"

"Yes, there is a twist. After one year we hope to see your entire service becoming independent of the Colorado office—that includes your deputies' salaries, Judge Hobart, and your office/jail rental."

"Fair enough, an appropriate challenge. Now let's meet with the Belchers."

"Nice to see you again Furman. Hannah, this is Furman and Laura Belcher, and this is my wife, Hannah." After small talk, Jake asked the first question. "Why would you consider leaving Colorado and moving to Texas?"

"Several reasons. My boys need work and you have a crop farm which is what they want to do. Laura wants a sense of community as well as living outside of town. We all want a Lutheran community to worship in, and I feel comfortable working for you."

"Can you work with a black man, an Apache and a newbie out of Lawman School?"

"Why of course, you know me!"

"What is involved in moving you to New Braunfels?"

"I already have a buyer for my house, and they have their own furniture. It's worth only $600 and we have a small savings of $500. What can we get with that money in your town."

"Your lodging will cost you nothing for one year. If you decide to stay at the end of one year, we'll talk about you buying your home. You will be in the fourth homestead east of my ranch and only four miles away from us and five miles west of town. It has no furnishings except for kitchen cabinets, cooking stove, kitchen sink with hand pump well and one parlor heating stove. It has one bedroom and an office on the first floor and three small bedrooms upstairs. The barn has its own hand pump well. It comes with ten acres which we'll get fenced in and separated in a garden and coral for your horses. Here is a bank voucher for $200 which will pay for transporting all your earthly belongings to New Braunfels by railroad boxcar. I will also arrange with Bromley Freighting to pick up all your stuff at the railroad yard and bring things to your new home. Again, this homestead is empty, bring everything you own because you'll need it since the house and barn are quite large."

Hannah was very observant and saw Laura tearing, as she asked, "what is wrong Laura?" "There is nothing wrong, it's just that Furman has dedicated his life for 20 years and we never had a helping hand. It's true that we supported ourselves and we managed, but this is the first time, thanks to you, that something great is happening to us."

Furman adds, "thanks, you know I'll have your back." "As will I!"

The last interview was with the newbie, Walt Garrett. "Hello, I'm Marshal Jake Harrison and this is my wife Hannah. You have great recommendations from you instructors at the Lawman School and from Captain Ennis. Now tell me, why would you want to live in New Braunfels?"

"I'm from Dallas where my family lives. It's more natural to make my bones as a US Marshal in a neutral community."

"Can you work with an experienced marshal, a black man and an Apache Indian?"

"I can work with anyone and will always have their backs."

"What do you know."

"I've been a bounty hunter, I'm financially independent and school trained in lawman work, but I don't have experience as a lawman. I am secure in my fast draw and other than that, I'm eager to get to work."

Hannah had only one question, "do you know who my husband is?"

"Yes Ma'am, Marshal Harrison is well known as a bounty hunter, Lawman School student, a jungle warfare expert, a successful leader of a Marshal squad as well as a large rancher and crop farmer."

Jake's last question was, "do you have any questions or something to add?"

"I admit that I have a lot to learn, but at least I know that you will guide me properly. In return, I'll work hard and always keep your interest and orders as the prime directive."

"Great, you're hired. You will have free housing in the jail's private room. As a newbie you will have the same salary and benefits as any other deputy. In addition, if we make arrests of wanted outlaws, you will share in the bounty rewards. In return for two meals a day at Bessie's diner, you will be our overnight jailer as your bed is already in the jail's office.

As a newbie, we will provide you with the extra firearms that is customarily used as a lawman, and that includes a horse stabled at Werner's livery. Welcome aboard, see you in New Braunfels within a week. Until Furman Belcher arrives, you'll be working with my good friend, Willie Irving."

***

That evening, Hannah got all gussied up for a formal supper with the Gibsons and an evening at the Hill theater. Arriving in the lobby, the Gibson's were already waiting for them. The Gibsons stood and Clifton introduced his wife as Josie. After a few social words, Hannah grabbed Josie's arm and escorted them to the magnificent Claymore's Ruby Restaurant.

Hannah started, "how strange life can be. You know Sylvia Adams and Jake has met her husband Max. I hear you want to leave the city and come back to Texas. Are you hoping to move to Alamo where Sylvia lives or Austin where your family lives?"

"Actually, I only have a sister with her family

that live in Austin. All my high school friends have moved away. Sylvia is too busy with her canning enterprise and moving there would be counterproductive. So, I'm hoping that we could live in-between the two so we can visit my friend and family by train. Clifton has no living family, so there is no pull to settle in any specific place. I plan to start a commercial vegetable garden and sell my produce in town. And, New Braunfels would be an ideal location, so, let's see how the business meeting goes between our husbands, heh"

Over two ice cold beers, Clifton started. "My three week's sojourn to prosecute Banfield, Beltzer and Klaus gave me an exposure to your town, and I was comfortable with what I saw. Now, tell me what you know about the job."

"As you know, this is a joint venture to prosecute district and federal cases. You know Judge Aiken and you'll appreciate Judge Hobart's no-nonsense approach. The pay is $200 per month, split between the two judicial systems. They will also pay your livery fees to keep a horse stabled during the day, and they allow an extra $40 allowance per month if you have a wife. You need to provide your own lodging, meals, transportation and personals. Judge Aiken has already supplied a legal library which will give you free access. Of course, you'll have your own office on the second floor of the courthouse which houses legal offices."

"I can afford to buy two horses and a buggy, but housing will be a problem. As a Captain Ennis' employee, I only amassed a savings of $800 over the past five years. Josie really needs 5 acres to make a commercial garden which means finding a rental in the country that is not too far from my work, and mercantiles for her produce."

"Not an issue. I just purchased four 10-acre homesteads with a house and barn. We'll divide the ten acres into two fenced in paddocks of five acres—one for her garden and one for a horse corral."

"Wow, that's a lot of real-estate; I don't know if we can afford all that?"

"Not going to cost you a penny. It's rent free for one year as long as you are willing to commit to our community for this year. Should you choose to stay, we'll talk about buying the homestead."

"Why are you doing this?"

"For two reasons. The first, I saw you in action during those three weeks and I know you're a good man—and one does what is necessary to keep a good man. The second, and most important reason, is right in front of your eyes."

"I'm not following you."

"Look at our wives. Hannah desperately needs and wants a friend and I suspect that Josie has the same need. I'll do anything to give my wife this very important social contact."

Clifton was in a deep pensive trance but finally spoke, "OMG, you are so correct, and you have a deal. We'll be here in two weeks." Josie heard the news and, along with Hannah, jumped for joy.

After a full course meal to include, spinach salad, filet mignon with mushroom sauce, baked potato, fresh roasted mixed vegetables and a cheesecake dessert with coffee; the two couples headed out to the Hill Theater. The comedy was hilarious, and the laughter helped increase the bond between the four individuals.

That evening, Hannah expressed her thanks to her perceptive husband, "you knew I needed female companionship. Now I'll have your mom, Josie, Furman's wife Laura and possibly Willie's girlfriend."

***

CHAPTER 2

THE SOUTH TEXAS MARSHAL SERVICE

During the long ride home, the duo covered several subjects. Utmost on Hannah's mind was how to prepare these homesteads for the new tenants. They finally agreed that Hannah would hire a cleaning service to clean the ranch houses. Since all the homesteads were empty of furnishings except the kitchen stove, sink, hand pump well and one or two heating stoves, they decided to contact the Gibsons and Belchers to find out what they were bringing for furniture. Whenever items were not coming in, Jake would order these items and have them delivered in the houses. They also agreed that basic supplies were needed before the tenants arrived. This included firewood, a larder with basic staples, and hay/oats for the horses.

Each of the four households had specific needs. Josie needed her 5-acre garden plowed and tilled to planting readiness. Willie, as a bachelor, had no furniture and the basic three-room would be supplied to include kitchen table/chairs, parlor furniture and one bedroom furnishings. Like Willie, Clayton had nothing, and the three-room basic furniture would be provided. The Belchers would have the abandoned 2-acre garden tilled back to life, the chicken coop upgraded, and 50 mixed breed layers would be added. In addition, all four 10-acre plots would be fenced. The corral was with barbwire and the garden was fenced with 2-inch webbed hardware to keep varmints out.

Arriving home, they set out to make this all happen. The decision was made as to who would get which homestead. Starting east of the Harrison's barn, Clayton would have the first homestead since he needed to be in walking distance to the ranch and easily accessible to the cowhands and cropboys. The next homestead would go to the Gibsons. This would make Josie's ride to Hannah and Clifton's ride to town as short as possible. The third would be Willie's place since it had a smaller ranch house. The fourth and largest ranch house would be the Belchers homestead with the three extra bedrooms on the second floor.

The next morning Jake went to the courthouse to arrange for a Marshal Service jail, office and sleep quarters for the jailer. Jake made contact with Hollis Bradshaw, joint clerk for Judges Aiken and Hobart.

"Hollis, in establishing a US Marshal Service, we're going to need a jail, office and sleeping quarters for one jailer. Can you help me out?"

"The first floor only has the courtroom that is shared by our two judges. That leaves two good size empty rooms. One could be the jail room with three cells and the other could be the marshal's office and sleep quarters. The two rooms could easily be connected. The square footage is presently available at $30 dollars a month which includes hot and cold-water plumbing, water closet and coal for heat. The office door will open to the outside Main Street and your horses can be stabled in the barn behind the courthouse."

"We'll take it. Would you arrange to have a connecting door installed and get the blacksmith to build three cells, two small and one large. And, have those cell windows removed and closed up with bricks."

"I'll arrange everything. I happen to know that the blacksmith is low on work and will likely start tomorrow if not today. Cass Construction will make your changes within a week."

"Perfect. Judge Hobart has a budget for such expenses and will cover all expenses. Let me know when we can take occupancy."

***

The next ten days were filled with moving-in activities. The Belchers and Gibsons arrived with wagon loads of furniture and personal belongings. Clayton and four cowhands were present to help unload Bromley's freight wagons and help them to move in. Laura and Josie, beyond belief, were pleased with the homesteads. The houses were clean and fully stocked. The purchased furniture also arrived and set out in Clayton and Willie's homes. Finally, the Harrisons met Clayton's fiancé, Sandra Kinney as well as Willie's girlfriend, Camilla Winters. Sandra and Camilla were surprised at Hannah's reception with her intense hugs and sincere welcome to their new home.

The Harrisons arrived with a house-warming gift for each of the homes. Bromley's wagons arrived with four manually operated washing machines with rollers to wring out the clothes. The ladies were in heaven since none of them had ever seen such machines. For the next few days, all the new occupants made their final purchases and settled in their new homes.

Jake went to town and ordered several items that the Marshals would need. He also set up an account at the telegraph office with a $50 deposit. The account would pay the messenger two-bits for delivering a telegram or a message to Jake, and pay for any answer being brought back by the messenger.

With everyone settled in, Hannah decided to have their first communal dinner. She prepared a 25-pound turkey with all the fixings to include homemade stuffing, mashed potatoes, carrots, giblet gravy, a 15-pound ham for those who prefer an alternative to turkey, and a huge store bought cake to serve 30 people. The attendees included the senior Harrisons, Clayton and Sandra, Willie and Camilla, the Belchers with three sons, the Gibsons, the Wolfgangs, Rocky and Red Flower, Walt Garnett and the Newmanns.

The event was a congenial affair. Camilla and Josie were clearly happy to mingle with everyone present. Hannah heard Camilla whisper to Willie, "are these people color blind? Don't they realize that white folks don't associate with our kind?" Willie answered, "better get used to it. These are good people who don't believe in segregation. You won't have to work hard to be accepted; and even become friends with all the ladies, especially Hannah."

For two hours, the visiting continued and when everyone was introduced, dinner was called. Hannah, with Erna and Helga's help, had prepared the food and decorated the massive extended dinner table. Herman was asked to say grace. He did the usual religious invocation but added, "and we should thank Jake and Hannah for their generosity and unrelenting friendship." The meal was a success, and with plenty of coffee and tea, the lemon cake from a local bakery was served.

***

Several days later, Jake called the first meeting of the South Texas US Marshal service. Jake started the meeting. "First off, let's talk about firearms. I expect each of you to have a pistol, Win 73, Win 76, a 1897 pump shotgun, a sawed-off double barrel 10 gauge shotgun in a backpack, a 41 caliber derringer and one 44 caliber Bulldog in a shoulder holster for undercover work. If you need any of these, go to Blackwell's gun shop and pick them up at my cost. Plus, any ammo you need for all these guns."

"I expect each of you to have a pair of moccasins in your saddlebags. As for a uniform, we'll dress with a blue/grey hickory shirt, striped grey pants, a black vest, and a black hat. You can pick up these items in triples at Wolfgang's mercantile—also at my cost."

"In my barn, there are three extra-large saddlebags. One is for my jungle warfare paraphernalia, the second is for cooking utensils to include fire grate, lightweight frying pan and coffee pot. The third is for vittles which you will get out of my larder—half for a cold camp and half for a hot camp. On a manhunt or on the trail, I expect each of you to take one of these extra-large saddlebags."

"In your individual saddlebags you should include your shaving kit, ammo for each firearm, change of clothes and other personal items. I will always carry 50X binoculars, a compass, a sewing kit, bandages and carbolic acid to sterilize a wound. You are responsible to bring your own bedroll, rain duster, and I strongly recommend a winter coat because of the cold nights."

"Walt will be using the sleeping quarters in the office/jail. In return for his jailer services and night duty, he will get two free meals per day. The rest of us, on routine days, meals are on us. If on manhunts, any meals taken in diners will be paid by me."

"When delivering processes, the lead man must always have a backup man holding a shotgun. That's because it is very common for the recipient of bad news to attack or kill the messenger."

Every morning, Furman and Willie will meet at the office to get the assignments of the day. If I'm needed, you can send the telegraph messenger to get me or you'll have to come and get me yourselves."

"Rocky is hired help as needed. He is a capable rifleman and our designated tracker. He's paid on a daily basis and only works when we need him. Every day, he's the ranch's wrangler."

"Every squad needs a leader. When I'm not

present, Furman has the most experience and will be the lead man."

"We'll have plenty of time to cover other details as we work together. For now, remember that we are not to put our lives in danger in order to bring an outlaw to justice. I would appreciate it if you all acknowledged my basic rule—'if an outlaw goes for his gun, it's time to kill or be killed.' Any questions"

Furman started, "is practice ammo included?"

"Yes, and unlimited."

Walt asked, "do we buy our own horses"

"Let me clarify where the funds come from to provide you all these free items. When on a manhunt, any recovered monies that are not returnable are deposited in thirds to: my South Texas US Marshal Service account, the Colorado US Marshal Service, and Judge Hobarts account. This is for the next year since Captain Ennis is paying your salary, benefits and the Judge's budget. It is these local funds from my Marshal Service account that I use to pay your expenses. At the end of one year, if we are a successful entity, we will be totally independent of the Colorado US Marshal Service. Now to answer your question, yes, the Service will pay for your mounts."

Willie commented, "that's a huge goal for us to reach in one year. Do you really think we can become independent?"

"Without a doubt. Some of these outlaws carry years of stolen funds with them. They're on the move and don't use banks that they rob. It's downright stupid, but that's the way it is and it's to our advantage, heh!"

Walt asked, "who are we working for? Who's our boss?"

"You all work for me, yet the squad works for Judge Hobart most of the time. Again, if Captain Ennis gives us an assignment, we also work for him. To complicate matters, if Judge Aiken or Sheriff Bixby ask for our help, we will respond in the affirmative if at all possible. I presume that's clear as mud." Laughter and guffaws followed.

With no further questions, the meeting came to a close. "Rocky you are back at work as our wrangler till we need you. We all start working tomorrow and I'm certain that there are plenty of processes to deliver. I will work tomorrow with Walt, and you two alternate as backup and delivery man. See you tomorrow night at the office."

***

The next morning, Judges Hobart and Aiken were glad to dispense the overdue processes. Each team had four processes to deliver. Jake and Walt had two divorce decrees to dispatch for Judge Aiken and two of Hobarts Federal foreclosures. They rode to the first ranch and knocked at the front door. A rather scruffy rancher opened the door and spoke with an unpleasant tone, "who are you and what do you want?"

With Walt holding his sawed-off shotgun at the ready, Jake said, "I'm US Marshal Jake Harrison and I am serving you a divorce settlement. This is your third notice and if you don't appear in front of District Judge Aiken in two days, I'll be back to arrest you and throw you in jail. Is that clear?"

"What the hell, since when do we have local US Marshals?"

"This is our first day, and we're here to stay. If you don't show up to settle with your wife, it's going to suck to be you!"

"Since you put it that way, I'll be there."

The next process was similar except the rancher looked at the paper and hesitated. Jake recognized the fact that the rancher could not read, so Jack read the entire document. "This is your first notice . . . . and your presence in front of District Judge Aiken is requested in one week for a final financial divorce settlement and termination of your marriage."

"Well, I guess I pushed her to the breaking point, and I'll be there with a bank draft and will make things right."

The third process was a foreclosure. Jake explained that there were two types of foreclosures. He said, "one that is sad because the homesteader could not make a living despite working hard at it. The other is the rare free loader that lives on the homestead but doesn't work at it and never pays his mortgage." Now arriving at the first homestead, the house and barn were both in disrepair. There was trash all over the yard and the corral was falling apart. Jake said, "this is not going to be a an easy one. You need to present this one, but be ready. The recipient will either draw his gun on you or assault you. I'll be your backup, but I want you to handle whatever comes at you."

The team went to the front door and knocked. Walt said, "I need to speak to a Cranston Sylvester, I am US Deputy Marshal Walt Garnett." Minutes passed before the door opened, appearing was an ill kept man in a filthy union suit with a strong smell of alcohol on his breath. Walt started the conversation, "are you Cranston Sylvester?'

"Yeah, what is it, I haven't broken the law to deserve the law's poking in my life?"

"Sir, this is a judicially endorsed bank foreclosure and eviction. You are ordered off this homestead by noon tomorrow with your personal belongings, or you will be physically removed by the US Marshal Service. Is that clear?"

Sylvester's face turned red and his eyes showed his ire. Without any warning he sucker punched Walt in the mouth. Walt rebounded and landed a round punch to the man's nose and flattened it. Sylvester dropped to his knees and came up with a knife. Walt changed gears and planted his foot in Sylvester's crotch. The man bent over holding on to his cojones. Walt then told him what he thought of him. "You are the poorest excuse for a man I've seen. You're filthy and your breath smells like you breathe thru your butthole. This place is in shambles and I just can't believe the law can't throw you in jail. The bank will get shafted and all they can do is evict you." Despite the verbal thrashing, Sylvester stood straight and tried to head butt Walt. Walt ducked and landed several punches to the man's face till he collapsed. Walt then asked the man if there was anyone in the house.

"No, the wife and kids left a year ago to go back to Indiana. Help me up, I've had enough. I'll leave tonight."

"You'd better. We'll be back tomorrow at noon and if you're here we'll tie a rope around you and drag you to jail." Before Walt turned away, without warning, he grabbed the man's nose and unceremoniously straighten it. Sylvester let out a scream that impressed Jake.

The second Federal foreclosure was different. Jake was the presenter and knocking at the front door, the homesteader's wife opened the door. She wore a tattered dress and was surrounded by three children less than ten years of age. "How may I help you Marshal?"

"We're looking for Stan Washington, I presume he's your husband."

"Yes, Stan is in the barn."

"Stepping in the barn, Stan was mucking the stalls. "Hello Marshal, I suspect I know why you're here. I told Judge Hobart that I had a large crop of alfalfa and would be able to pay a portion of my overdue mortgage payments in one week. I guess that was not good enough, heh?"

"You've had some hard times have you?"

"Yeah, this is the first time in three years that the drought doesn't wipe out my 100 acres of alfalfa. Could I harvest the crop and then we'll leave and move on."

"How much land do you have??

"A half section or 320 acres of very fertile land. My plans three years ago were to expand each year, but that never happened with the drought."

"How much to you owe the Federal Government and local mercantiles."

"I owe Judge Hobart $379 on my half section mortgage and interest, and Herman Wolfgang $89. We've been living on our garden, eggs and deer meat since I just can't ask Herman for any more credit."

Jake then pulled out his wallet, filled out a paper, and signed it. "Here is a bank draft on my account for $2,000. Pay off your mortgage and your credit debt. Buy your family some food and clothes, and give your kids some candy and toys. Then hire some help, buy the necessary implements and cultivate 100 more acres. Plant a mixed crop of alfalfa, hay, oats, potatoes and sugar beets. Varying crops are a buffer against insects or droughts. And add a lean-to on your barn to store your crops."

Jake and Stan both turned to see where several gasps had come from. The culprits were Walt and the homesteader's wife. Stan hesitated and softly asked, "why would you do such a thing? We're nobody to you."

"You're not nobody. You are a hard-working man who has gone thru some bad times and you need a helping hand. Had you gone back to Herman's store; he would have included you in my Benefactor Fund. I only ask that you tell no one where the money came from, heh."

***

The next day, Jake and Walt were sent to collect overdue property taxes. A large rancher had been expanding his ranch. He added three sections of public lands at 50 cents an acre. The 1,900 acres had cost $950. By state law, he could get the land deeded to him with a deposit of $100. On top of that he had bought 100 young heifers worth another $2,000. The total purchases had left him cash poor and he hadn't paid his taxes for two years or paid any of the installments for his land purchase. Judge Aiken and Hobart issued a delinquent tax order and overdue payments to the county. The order demanded immediate payment, or the ranch would be put up for tax sale per county law.

Jake thought the demands were excessive and wondered if there was more to this than appeared, so he went to see Judge Hobart.

"I'm having trouble serving this demand for tax sale. Is there more to the story?"

"Yes, this man is well off and everyone knows it. He hates the county government and has decided that he can disregard the law and refuse to pay his share of taxes due. Other ranchers are coming to the town clerk and claiming that if the Circle G ranch can get away from paying taxes, then they should be afforded the same benefit. This cannot continue."

"Very good, we'll take care of this today. I guarantee you we'll be back with all back payments and even taxes for next year."

Arriving at the Circle G ranch, the housekeepe greeted and escorted them to Grant

G Galvin's office. Standing at the man's desk, Jake saw a well-dressed rancher writing with his left hand, which was next to a pistol on the desk.

The rancher was not acknowledging their presence, so Jake asked, "excuse me sir, but are you Grant G. Galvin?" With no answer forthcoming, Jake added, "it is customary and polite for the person being addressed to at least look up and visually make contact with the person speaking!"

Galvin quickly stood up with both hands on the desk, spotted the US Marshal badge and said, "I don't care who you are, I'll speak to you when I'm good and ready. Now shut up and wait."

As Galvin sat down to continue writing, Jake pulled out his pistol and slammed the grip onto the top of Galvin's right hand. The impact smashed some bones and drew blood. Galvin screamed in pain as his bug-eyes fixed on his crushed hand. At the same time, Walt was startled and ended up taking a step backwards.

Galvin yelled out, "I'm going to kill you for

this." As he went for his pistol with his left hand, Jake reacted. He stomped on his left hand with his own left hand and used his right hand to lift and push back Galvin's index and middle finger completely backwards. Galvin screamed and groaned in pain as he collapsed on his desktop with his two dislocated fingers pointing straight up.

Galvin eventually spoke with a shaky voice, "why did you do this?"

"First of all, I can't stand a man who disrespects the badge of a US Marshal. Secondly, you are an arrogant snob who needed this afront to get your attention."

Jake then turned to Walt and said, "watch the door, Galvin's cowboys will be rushing the house to see what all the screaming was about."

As expected, four cowhands rushed the front door only to walk right in front of Walt's sawed-off shotgun. "This is not your fight boys, get out or you'll die right here."

Seeing their boss bent over his desk with an apparent busted hand and holding his left with two deformed fingers, they quietly stepped back to the porch to wait the outcome.

“Now Mister Galvin, listen carefully. I have an order from Judge Aiken to collect two years of back property taxes and one year of current taxes. That total comes to $1,850 with back interest. I also have an order from Judge Hobart demanding full payment of overdue installments of $850. That comes to $2,700. Now open the safe and pay up.”

“I can’t you idiot, both my hands are busted. Have my foreman, on the porch, come in to open the safe.”

With the safe open, $3,000 were withdrawn. Galvin yells out, “the amount was $2,700, what’s the extra $300 for?”

“To cover our fees coming out here, the judge’s fees, meals for you for a month and your doctor bills.”

“What do you mean, meals for a month?”

“Oh, I forgot to mention. You’re under arrest for aggravated assault of a US Marshal with a firearm. That’s an automatic jail sentence of 30 days. And a trial or a lawyer are not necessary.

It's the law. You know, the laws that you didn't follow and ended up this way, heh?"

Riding in town with Galvin's hands manacled, his right hand bandaged, his left fingers in a strange configuration, the message was clear. Jake finally said, "this man is going to jail for 30 days for assaulting an officer and not paying his taxes. Better pay up if you are in arrears, heh."

***

That evening, Jake and Hannah met with Clayton who had some important news. Clayton started, "I have a friend who told me that the Federal Land Agency is putting up public land for sale east of town for the first time. The sale begins tomorrow at the town clerk's office, and they are selling the open range north of your four sections. The land is going for 50 cents an acre and we need to increase our acreage. With almost 850 head of cattle, we've been using the open range north of your fenced in four sections. Keep in mind that it takes 5 acres to support one cow or steer, so your 2,500 only has 2,000 fertile acres with good grass, and that only supports 400 heads. We need to buy land before someone else buys it and fences you out."

"Ironically, I found out about this public land sale when I arrested Grant Galvin yesterday. Apparently, the public land sales have all been 'far east' of town till now. How many acres should I buy?"

"The minimum of the four sections north of your own four sections. That is 2,560 acres or $1,280. Now if you agree, we can start fencing in these new acres. The boys don't have much work this winter except for maintenance, delivering hay and spreading manure. I can spare at least eight men till spring and we can do a lot of fencing in the next months. I'll even hire the Belcher boys to help."

"Go ahead and order your supplies of posts, barbwire and staples. Your boys can start digging holes till the supplies arrive. I'll be at the town clerk's office in the morning when the office opens. If you want to add all of your crop team early, go ahead and do so. The more fencing we do by spring the better off we'll be."

That evening, Hannah asked what Jake's long-term goals were regarding oil and ranching. Jake answered, "my plate is quite full, with managing a ranch, a squad of US Marshals, and keeping a wife satisfied and happy. I don't think I want to get involved with drilling for oil myself. Instead, I'd rather buy more land before the price goes up."

"Actually, I'm thinking of buying land between the ranch and town along the roadside. Plus, range land north of that, north of us, and north of Dieter Klaus' land."

Hannah said, "Ok, let's add this all up. The one section between us and town will go for $1 an acre since it abuts town. The section north of that one will also go for $1 an acre. So that comes to $1,280 for those two sections. You've already said that the four sections north of our ranch come to $1,280. Now add four sections north of Klaus's land for another $1,280. That comes to $3,840. Which will now give us ten sections more than our four sections. So that is adding 6,400 acres to our present 2,560 acres. I would say that owning +-10,000 acres makes us a large ranch by present Texas standards, heh."

"Yes, this is still cheaper than digging a well. So, by extending our range for cattle, it allows us more land to cultivate next to the roadside and our storage sheds. Keep in mind, I really want to expand the crop business into a commercial enterprise."

"Done, now it's time to satisfy this wife, as you so stated. A happy wife is a happy life, heh."
"Yes dear!"

The next morning Jake and Hannah were sitting on the boardwalk waiting for the town clerk. Arriving on the scene he asked, "good morning folks, arc you waiting for me?"

"Yes Sir. We want to be the first to purchase your public lands going for sale by the Feds."

"Great, let's look at the map surrounding the Circle H ranch."

"Hannah point to the wall map and says, "we want these two sections west of us, these four sections north of us and these four sections north of Klaus' land."

"The land between you and town is $1 an

acre and the remainder is 50 cents an acre and the total comes to $3,840."

Jake adds, "now add the taxes for all this land and our ranch for the coming year."

"The grand total is $4,649."

Jake paid with a bank draft and then asked that the deeds be prepared in both their names. Before they left the office, they walked out with three separate deeds. With the deed done, the Harrisons decided to go to Bessie's Diner for breakfast. As they arrived at the diner, they were surprised to see the name had changed to Natalie's Diner. Stepping inside, the waitress looked familiar to Jake.

"What can I get you?" Hannah said, "coffee, scrambled eggs, home fries, toasted bread and bangers." "And what about you, sir?" "Same, but don't I know you Ma'am?" "Yes, you do. Think about where we met, and after I put your order in, I'll be back and refresh your memory."

Hannah added, "is this one your dalliances before we met?"

"Now woman, you know you're my only

dalliance. No, I just can't place her, but I know I've met her before."

"Ok, time to fess up." "Sorry, I can't place you and I hope our past encounter was not an unpleasant one."

"It was in Trinidad, Colorado. There was a bank robbery at the Merchant's Bank and an innocent bystander was killed. That was my husband. You were a young bounty hunter and went after the bank robbers. When you returned with the killer robbers and the money, you gave me $2,000 of your own money as a measure of justice for the victims. I used the money to buy a diner and did well. When my mom got ill in New Braunfels, I sold the diner and moved here to be with her. Bessie had this diner for sale, and I bought it. Bessie is now the cook and I'm the waitress. Small world isn't it?"

As they were talking, Walt Garnett rushed in and accidentally bumped into Natalie. "Oh, excuse me Ma'am, I have a message for Marshal Harrison."

Natalie smiled and added, "Marshal heh, I

didn't see your badge hidden under your vest. And who is this lady?"

"This is my lovely wife, Hannah."

"And who are you sir."

"I'm Marshal Harrison's deputy. And your name is?"

"Natalie." They shook hands and seemed to spend a long time shaking and looking at each other. Hannah interrupted them and said that Bessie was waiting for them to move so she could deliver their breakfast.

Finally, Jake asked Walt what the urgent message was. "Oh, Judge Hobart has a problem he wants to discuss with you, ASAP."

"Ok, we'll be there after breakfast."

Hannah added, "Isn't this diner where you've been getting your meals"

"Yes, I missed breakfast today, but with that new owner, I'll be here for supper, for sure!"

***

CHAPTER 3

HANNAH JOINS THE TEAM

Judge Hobart greeted the Harrisons and said, "good morning, thank you for coming so quickly."

"Normally, it would have taken longer to respond, but today we were already in town. So, tell us what this is all about."

"Rustling has taken on a new twist with the development of refrigerated railroad boxcars."

"Refrigerated cars? Please bring us up to snuff about refrigeration."

"This is the 1890's and Texas has several ice producing plants that is used to keep boxcars near freezing temperatures. A 100-pound block of ice will melt down in three hours if the outside temp is 70 degrees. This gives the railroad two hours to get to the next ice plant or refrigerated warehouse. Yes, we now have refrigerated warehouses that use either ether/naphtha or water/ammonia gaseous contraction to generate refrigeration. Soon, we'll have true refrigeration boxcars if they are not already available."

"Anyways, this is what is happening in San Antonio. Rustlers are forming fence cutting squads to enter their wagons into fenced in pastures or even the open range. They work as a gang and butcher full size cows or steers during the middle of the night. They partially pull the hide to harvest the four quarters and the backstrap. The remainder of the carcass and hide are left to the predators. The meat is then lightly salted to preserve it, the harvested beef is covered with tarps, and rushed to the railroad yard by daybreak. The meat buyers weigh each quarter and pay cash by the pound. The sides of beef are then stored in the refrigerated boxcars and shipped off every day by noon to the nearest refrigerated warehouse."

"To continue, the meat buyers don't have a brand they can use to check for stolen cattle. So, all fresh quarters are accepted by the buyers who represent the Midwest meat packers."

"How is this a Federal issue?"

"Because this involves the inter-state transfer of stolen goods. Now, if this problem continues, the ranchers will eventually figure out that they can place a claim against the Feds for financial compensation. This has been going on for some time and it needs to stop for eventually it will affect every rancher in the state."

"Well, we have to agree with you, but it seems this will be a difficult case to crack. I'll have to go to San Antonio to do some detective work before I bring the squad in to make the arrests."

"Just be careful, this is a gang of rough gunfighters who face a hanging for rustling activities in Texas. My sources suspect, according to the tracks, that you will be dealing with eight outlaws. Since we have no proof of their activities, you'll have to catch them in the act."

That evening after supper Hannah brought up an interesting dilemma. "Jake, I have writer's cramp. I wanted to write a fiction about wagon trains out west, but my class instructor says that I should write my first book about what I know. Well, what do I know? I know about chickens, living in New Braunfels, and reading books. Now since I met you, I know about ranching, self-defense with firearms, and how to function as a lawman. This is compounded by my reading the four bounty hunting fictions by Swanson, Harnell, Adams and the latest by Randy McWain."

Jake interrupts her and says, "and where is this leading to?"

"I want to write a western fiction in our times about being a bounty hunter who turns into a US Marshal. Just like you. So, what I need is to go over your capers as a bounty hunter and your time as a Marshal. In addition, I need more first-hand experience, and I want to join your team on this caper in San Antonio, as well as the many other assignments you will have in the months to come."

"What, and put your life in danger, these are dangerous outlaw gunfighters and not your clucking chickens. When confronted by us, they want to kill us."

"I know all that, but it's still my choice to put myself in harm's way. Besides, you know I can handle my pistol and now the new pump 1897 shotgun. Heck, I can even slam-fire it with accuracy."

"What in blazes is slam-firing a pump shotgun?"

"It's a method of rapid firing a pump that I've been practicing with your deputies. It's simple really, just keep your trigger depressed like you do when you fan-fire your pistol. With the trigger depressed, every time you pull the slide forward, it automatically fires. The trick is to point-shoot and hit the target. With slam-firing, there is no time to aim."

"Oh really!" Jake spent a moment in silence and finally said, "Ok, well try it on this caper. I expect you to be the tail-man on all encounters, and you will not participate in any all-out face to face gunfight. When you get pregnant, the deal is off. Agree?"

"Agree, so since I'm to be your tail-man, how about 'a piece of tail' tonight, heh." "For sure, Ma'am!"

The next day, Jake and Hannah took the train to San Antonio. To be close to the train yard, they took a room in the railroad's hotel, the Grand Cramer and Restaurant. That evening they had a fine supper of red wine, rare filet mignon, baked potatoes, boiled beets, fresh buttered sourdough bread and a dessert of their favorite rice pudding over coffee and tea. Afterwards, they attended a musical play at the Hill Theatre. Getting back to their hotel, Jake was beginning to help Hannah undress when she said, "we've been married several months and every time we make love, I feel like I'm going to pass out after our nirvana."

"Why is that, maybe you should ask Doc Craven what that means."

"I did. He said that you turn me on so much that, when I reach my nirvana, too much blood rushes to my privates. This causes a drop in blood flow to my brain which makes it feel like I'm going to pass out."

"So, does that mean that I should simmer down stimulating you?"

"Oh no, I said I feel like passing out, not actually going out. Besides my new lady friends, Josie and Camilla, call that the 'afterglow.' Now let's see how much my glow will light up the room!"

The next morning, after a replenishing breakfast, the duo went to see the railroad yard manager. The man was pleasant and volunteered to share what he knew on the matter. "My job is to get my men to load the beef and keep the car at 40° F or lower. The refrigerated car belongs to Weston Meat Packers out of Kansas. Their buyer stays in the Cramer Hotel and his name is Fabian Applegate. He can usually be found in the Cattlemen's Club which is on the first floor of the same hotel. He's the man to talk to for more information on the matter."

The Duo headed to the Cattlemen's Club and were directed to the table where a man was going over the day's invoices. Hannah walked up to the man and said, "excuse me, but are you Mister Fabian Applegate?"

"Yes Ma'am, what can I do for you?"

"We would like to talk to you about the beef you buy every morning."

"Well, I see that you are US Marshals, and I'd be happy to tell you what I know."

Jake asked, "can you describe the process you go thru every day?"

"Every morning from 7—11AM, I am at the loading platform. I examine the meat, and if it's clean, fresh, and lightly salted; I pay cash by the pound for hind quarters, front quarters and backstraps. The source of the meat is not my business, but I recognize many respectable ranchers that need an immediate inflow of cash short of shipping a portion of their herd to market. I deal with ranchers within 20 miles of San Antonio. If some of these ranchers are rustlers, there is no way for for me to tell. That's all I can say."

Hannah added, "we are looking for a gang of eight rustlers. Could it be possible that they send a different man to sell their stolen beef and rotate the men every eight days?"

Applegate was noted to be thinking of the question. "Yes, I think you have something there. There is a heavy-duty freight wagon that delivers a full load of pieces, usually consistent with 8—12 animals. And you're correct, it's a different man each day."

"That is who we are after."

"Well, I represent a legitimate company, and if these are rustlers, I will do my best to help you out. Why don't you come to the loading platform tomorrow and hide in the background. When the wagon arrives, I'll take my hat off to signal you. I'll continue with the sale and I'll expect you to take over once the suspected rustler leaves the yard."

The next morning, Jake and Hannah were dressed in trail riding clothes with their rented horses. They were watching Applegate at work. It was clear when that heavy freight wagon arrived at 7AM with a full load of beef. The signal came and the Duo waited for the suspect to leave. Then they stepped up to Applegate and thanked him for his help. Applegate added, "that load represented eleven animals and I paid them $240. That's $30 per day per man. Not bad for an easy day's work."

The Duo started following the wagon. With the flat landscape, they stayed over three miles behind the wagon—just far enough to still see the massive wagon but their smaller silhouette would be difficult to spot by the wagon driver. Jake then spoke, "assuming they started working their dirty deed at midnight, they would have spent an hour lassoing their catch, two hours to butcher and salt the quarters. So, by 3AM, they would be on route to the train yard. That's four hours of travel time and at 3 mph, that means they were twelve miles away. Now, more than likely they have a cabin at least six miles from town. That would allow them access to town for supplies and entertainment. As soon as we spot the cabin, we'll hold back. We'll head to town and telegraph the squad to come by train, with their guns and horses, ASAP."

That evening, the 9PM Express train arrived from New Braunfels with the four-man squad. After all the firearms and horses were unloaded, Furman asked what the plan was. Jake explained everything they had discovered and where the cabin was located. "Load up with water and food for a cold camp and we'll wait at the cabin and follow them when they take off with the freight wagon. From there, we'll develop the final attack plan when we see where they are working."

With a moonlit night, they arrived at the cabin within an hour. At 10PM, the rustlers took off. Seven riders were moving ahead as the wagon was slowly following along. The squad was following the wagon from a safe distance. By midnight, the wagon arrived where a dozen animals were tied to a tree awaiting slaughter.

The Marshals were looking at the slaughter site from 150 yards away. Jake gave his final attack plans. "Hannah, you're going to sit on that knoll with a Win 76. You'll set your scope at 150 yards and shoot off cross-sticks. Your job is to spot that guard sitting on his horse with a rifle in hand. The moment you see him pull up his rifle and aim, he's going to shoot one of us, so you need to take him out immediately. Any questions?" "Yes, do I watch what you guys are doing or do I only watch the guard?" "It doesn't matter what we are doing, just watch that guard and take him out before he shoots us." "Got it."

To the squad, "we're going to make our way thru the trees and once in the open field, we'll have about 50 yards to cover at a full run with our shotguns in hand. Rocky, you keep your rifle in hand. Once we start running, the skinners will be busy and won't be too close to their rifles, which will be left on their horse or in the wagon. We should be able to get in their faces before they get armed. Any questions or alternatives to this plan?" All the heads turned in the negative.

The squad made their way thru the trees and once they all gathered at the tree-line, Jake gave the order and the squad sprinted ahead.

Meanwhile, Hannah had the scope on the guard. Nothing was happening until suddenly his face changed, he pulled up his rifle and was about to take aim. Hannah never hesitated, she had a good hold of the rifle and quickly squeezed the trigger when the scope's crosshairs came to the guard's chest. In that instant, Hannah saw a puff of dust on the guard's shirt and the guard was then knocked clear off his horse. As a response to the gun's recoil, the gun recoiled upward and rearward. The cross-sticks fell to the ground as Hannah was pushed backwards and lost her balance from her one knee on the ground. As she landed on her butt, she found herself looking around to see if anyone had seen her fall on her rear-end. Realizing that her squad was running to the slaughter, she pulled her rifle up and saw that the guard's horse was standing without a rider. Looking around, she found the guard on the ground, and realized that she had done her job.

The squad was at a full run and at 25 yards from the wagon, Jake saw a rustler grab a rifle out of the wagon. Before he could decide how to respond, a rifle shot was heard. Jake looked to the side and saw Rocky bring his rifle down as the Rustler collapsed to the ground. The squad then arrived and placed all six men under arrest, and immediately manacled their hands and feet.

Out of nowhere, hoofbeats were heard and four riders arrived at a full gallop. "Well, I guess we're too late, we're from the Slash V Ranch and we were riding the range trying to catch these thieves."

"They had already slaughtered four steers and two men were working on each steer. Why don't you take four of their horses and bring the meat to your ranch and share it with your neighbors. Also, keep the four horses as partial restitution. We'll take two horses, their guns and the wagon to haul the rustlers back to San Antonio. Oh, and pass the word to the ranchers who lost animals. If we find the money they have collected from this caper, we'll return the funds to them. Just have them telegraph a claim to Judge Hobart in New Braunfels."

By daylight, the wagon full of rustlers arrived at the city marshal's office—minus the pocket cash of $479. The city marshal, Eb Brisco, informed the Marshals that the Cattlemen's Association had placed a $5,000 reward for the rustler's capture. The funds would be available today at the Cattlemen's Bank.

After getting a full breakfast at Sandy's diner, the squad went back to the rustler's cabin to find a money stash. They ransacked every nook and cranny in the house, barn and privy, but without any luck. Standing in the cabin, Rocky said, "look at stovepipe damper, it's in the closed position. Isn't that strange?" Suddenly all hands were on the stovepipe.

Separating the first section revealed four metal tins full of greenbacks. The counted total came to $3,375. These funds would be given to Judge Hobart to pay back the robbed ranchers' claims.

Getting back into town, Marshal Brisco handed out a $5,000 bank voucher. Jake went in the bank to cash in the voucher. He then distributed $833 to each squad member, including Hannah. Hannah objected to the distribution. She tried to point out that she was simply a squad observer as research for her first book. No one would buy it, and Furman pointed out how her perfect shot had likely saved one of the squad's bacon. She relented and smiled her thanks.

Rocky looked perplexed, holding all this money. "I don't deserve and cannot accept all this money. I work for $55 with Red Flower, and that is good pay for Indians."

Every squad member was trying to speak at one time. Jake broke it up and said, "Rocky, you are part of this squad, and I know no one else could have put that outlaw down, shooting on a full run. Now, every time you come out with us; you are putting your life on the line. That's what you're paid for. Now, this is your money to do as you wish. If you want to give it to your family in the reservation, that's your choice, but it's your money." "Ok, I buy new hides to cover my teepee, buy Red Flower her own sawed-off shotgun, will keep a small reserve in the bank and give the rest to my family in the reservation. Thank you!"

***

The next day, Jake sent a telegram to Judge Hobart. It was agreed that he would travel to San Antonio and hold a trial for the six surviving rustlers. Once this was arranged,

Walt and Willie would stay and arrange to rent a courtroom for the trial. Walt would be the court bailiff and Willie would be the court's guard. The remainder of the squad would return home.

That evening, after supper, the Duo sat in their parlor for personal and reading time. Hannah was sitting down with a writing pad on her lap. She started, "After our caper in capturing the rustlers, I'm ready to take notes on your own experiences—I need ideas before I start writing."

Jake knew that this day would come and had an idea. "I will describe the capers I set up but will not give names or locations involved since they hold no benefit to your book. My experiences will allow you to use the events in your fiction."

"That's just what I need. Go ahead and I'll try not to interrupt you unless there is something I don't understand."

Jake pulls out his notes and says, "I've made a list of a dozen capers that are worth mentioning."

1. "Securing a safe camp is paramount to surviving the night in a camp on the trail. It starts with a string surrounding the camp and also includes. . . . . .all these extras."
2. "Going solo against a large gang is suicide unless you can even the odds. I've had to pick-off gang members from afar using my long range rifle and . . . . it was necessary to survive and fight another day."
3. "Dealing with an expected bank robbery, I had to dress as a bank teller in order to. . . . . .bring an end to a killer gang."
4. "Protecting a stagecoach from a marauding gang requires special handling. I protected the jehu and the shotgun guard with steel plates as I hid in the boot with several loaded shotguns. . . . . .with drastic results."
5. "Aborting a train robbery on the passenger car required protecting the passengers while putting down the outlaw. . . . . .and that was how I

saved the life of a high ranking railroad executive and why he owes me a favor."

Hannah's eyebrows went up and said, "yes, it seems you have referred to this situation when you had crazy ideas of setting up a rail head to the ranch, heh?"

"Hu'um. Remind me to send a telegram to start this process. Moving on!"

6. "Making a safe arrest of outlaws in a public saloon.. . . . . .it requires a backup."
7. "The dreaded 'face to face' gunfight. . . . . always leads to utter devastation."
8. "Using a fanning fast draw to put down three outlaws. . . . . .is said to sound like a single shot!"
9. "Poisoning whisky with ipecac and a horse laxative. . . . . .has stinking but effective results."

Hannah gasped and said, "I'm nauseated just listening to you. Remind me to stay at home the day you use this caper!"

"You know a gasp is a sigh in reverse. Just to warn you, you'll be exposed to several new jungle warfare techniques, and you'll be gasping frequently."

10. "Booby trap an outlaw camp with bear traps and. . . . . .has a way of bringing outlaws to their knees."
11. "How two lawmen handle a known ambush. . . . . .requires precision responses with shotguns."
12. "Detective work can be required. . . . . .when the motive for murder is based on a case of the 'clap.'"

Hannah again gasped, "are you for real, a wire heated to 110° F inside the p---s! I'll write about the successful oral treatment with Balsam of Copiaba—if you don't mind, heh?"

"Well that's it for tonight. I think you can

start writing and take advantage of your writing instructor every Wednesday afternoon."

***

The next morning, their replenishing breakfast was interrupted with the sound of galloping hoofbeats. The rider arrived, stepped down and start pounding on the front door with his fists. Jake got up and opened the door only to see the angry face of Dieter Klaus.

Dieter forced his entry inside and yelled, "**YOUSTOLETHATPUBLICLAND UNDERMYNOSEANDYOU'R GOINGTOSELLITTOMENOW ORELSE!**

Jake took a moment and said, "stop your screaming, rambling and slow down. What is your problem and what do you want?"

"You stole that public land under my nose and you're going to sell it to me now, or else!"

"Yes, I bought some public land, what section were you interested in and why?"

"I want the two sections west of you that border the town line."

Hannah had now joined Jake and said, "again why those two sections?"

"Ok, here are the facts. When I arrived here, I was broke. It cost me a fortune to ship my oil drilling derrick and rotary drill to this ranch. I sold the 500 cattle for $10,000. I drilled three wells starting from east to west to the limit of my rig which is 1,300 feet. The first two wells were dry but the third, which is north of the four homesteads you bought from me, is showing some very oily stone chips. But I'm at the limit of 1,300 feet again. My head drilling man and geologist feel that the land bordering the town will come in at less than a thousand feet. That's why I want it. So, sign this quick claim deed and I'll pay you twice what you paid for it."

Jake looked at Hannah who shook her head sideways. "That is never going to happen. The land is not for sale. Now that you told me that land's potential, that is where I'll dig my well, if I so choose. So, if westward movement is so important. Why don't you buy some land west of town and dig your next well?"

"I've already tried that, but no one wants to sell. These dumb homesteaders put more value in potatoes than big money from oil."

"I suppose you could use the strong-arm method that your father tried. But that practice will no longer be tolerated, and let's not forget that this got your father hung!"

"Is that your final word?"

"Let me add, you need to be staked with funds so you can restart somewhere else. Unless I'm mistaken, you own six sections of land, or 3,840 acres with a ranch house, barn and bunkhouse. Land goes for 50 cents an acre but using $1 per acre plus buildings, I'll offer you $5,000 today and we'll go to the town clerk and transfer the deed. What do you say?"

Dieter was seemingly either fuming or considering the offer. Jake pushed the issue and said, "Dieter, you are at the end of your rope. If you don't take my offer, you'll have to declare bankruptcy in which case the feds will sell it at 10-20 cents on the dollar."

"I could always abandon the land and leave with my equipment."

"Yes, you could, but without a nest egg, you can't afford to pay the moving fees. Plus, without paying your property taxes for two years, the town will confiscate the property and put it up at auction for tax sale."

"There is another way, and you'll be begging me to accept my quick claim deed. I'm not destitute yet. I have enough money to pay for the alternative." Dieter turned and slammed the door on his way out. As he was seen leaving the access road, the telegraph messenger was seen coming their way.

"Hello Tommy, what have you got?"

"An emergency telegram requiring an immediate answer."

Jake read it and handed it to Hannah who read:

> **From Commandant Dutton Peabody STOP**
> **Denver Lawman School STOP**
> **Son, Dempsey, been kidnapped STOP**
> **Need your personal help STOP**
> **See Judge Hobart for details STOP**

Jake wrote one-line answer. "ON MY WAY, I'LL DO MY BEST"

After Tommy left, Hannah simply said, "let's change and head out to see Judge Hobart."

Arriving at the courthouse Marshal's office, Judge Hobart was waiting for the duo. "I have received a telegram from Captain Ennis requesting your help with this kidnapping. He also sent a copy of a local newspaper article about a Burlock gang of kidnappers. They are notorious for demanding high ransoms, but when they are paid, the victims are found dead. They finally left Colorado when the wanted rewards reached $7,000 for these four psychopathic killers. It is estimated that they have collected almost $10,000 in ransoms while operating in Colorado. Now, they have kidnapped Commandant Peabody's son and are demanding a ridiculous ransom of $50,000 or his son will be buried alive."

"How can the Commandant even come close to finding such a sum?"

"I guess you don't know, the Commandant comes from a big oil company and is worth much more than the asked ransom. He works as a Lawman School Commandant as a service to the lawman's profession. He doesn't even take a salary."

Hannah said, "wow, what a man. Tell us more, we need a lead to get started."

"Well, all we know is that Dutton is getting telegrams in Denver, at the Morse Drive office, from a man called Red Green—a likely made up name. Dutton's responses are sent to our own telegraph in town and addressed to a Mr. Red Green. Apparently, Ted in the telegraph office says that this same man comes in every other day to get his telegrams and sends a response to the Denver telegraph on Morse Drive the same day."

"Was this Dempsey living in the area, and how old is he?"

"Yes, he is only 18 and was working as a cowhand on a ranch west of town. I also want to add that the money has already been wired and has arrived at the Rancher's Bank. Plus, the Commandant and Missus are on their way from Denver. They could arrive as soon as tomorrow night. I also hate to add this, but I need to leave for the trial in San Antonio, and I need Walt and Willie as you promised me."

"Very good, go ahead and go to San Antonio with Walt and Willie, we'll manage with Furman and Rocky. Now, let's go see Ted and find out when this Red Green is expected to show up."

Walking in the telegraph office, Ted stood up and shook the Duos' hand. "I've been expecting you. When I notified Captain Ennis of my suspicions, he said you would be by to see me."

"With some help, we hope to capture these kidnappers and bring the young Peabody back home. Have you got anything new?"

"Yes, I received this telegram late yesterday, but it was sent to you. Read it."

Jake read it and said to Hannah, "it says that Dutton is to bring the package four miles west of town, and on the right, there will be a white flag. He is to place the package in a tin box behind the large boulder that the flag is leaning on."

Hannah adds, "when?"

"On Friday, which is three days from yesterday. Ted, do you know when Dutton Peabody is expected to arrive."

"He arrived last night and is at the railroad hotel next to the yard. He is waiting to see you."

"What can you tell us about this outlaw dude, and when can we expect him to pick up his telegram?"

"I expect him any time this morning. He rides a piebald horse with a chestnut gelding for a packhorse. The chestnut has two white boots on his forelegs. He wears two Colts with white grips. When he arrives in town, he comes here first and then steps across the street to pick up meat at the butcher and supplies at the mercantile next door. I suspect that this Red Green is looking for a confirmation that Peabody will be at the meeting point since this second telegram, similar to yours, also arrived last night.

"Ok, then I'll go and meet with Commandant Peabody. Hannah, you wait here, and when this dude shows up, just pretend you are sending a telegram. We need you to delay him while Rocky and Furman check his two horses' hoofs. We need to find some markings that will help Rocky tracking him to his den of kidnappers. When one of the boys waves his hat in the window, you'll know it's safe to leave. I will tell the boys that we'll all meet at the livery where our horses will be stabled out of view."

With things set up, Jake went to the hotel. The Commandant and his wife were waiting for Jake in the entrance parlor. Dutton stood up and shook Jake's hand. "Thank you for coming, I never thought we would ever meet again. Oh, excuse me, this is my wife Isabella."

The lady acknowledged Jake, but was hiding her teary eyes. "Sir, is there any hope of ever seeing our son again?"

"Ma'am, I have a very good team and if my plan works out, I'll have Dempsey back here tonight, the latest noon tomorrow. You certainly realize there are some risks, but I'm confident that we'll be successful. A prayer will help and will keep your mind occupied."

The Commandant added, "I've already wired

the $50,000 and I'm ready to pay the ransom if you decide that the rescue is too risky."

"This rescue is absolutely necessary. I'm sure I don't need to remind you how this gang deals with victims once the ransom is paid. Now, if you'll excuse me, I need to return to my team who is watching the telegraph office. If we're lucky, this Red Green, is expected soon to pick up your last confirmation message. We plan to track him to his camp and see how to proceed."

As Jack was leaving, he heard Isabella ask her husband what was meant about the kidnappers treating victims. It was clear that the Commandant was frank with his wife, as he heard her start wailing out loud.

Stepping out of the hotel, he started walking back to the telegraph office. Suddenly, he held up as he saw Rocky and Furman checking the pie bald horse's hoofs. Furman was then seen stepping on the boardwalk waving his hat and then he and Rocky turned around heading to the livery. Jake continued to watch, and true to form, Red Green picked up packages at the butcher shop and the mercantile. He then mounted his horse and headed out east of town. Getting back at the livery, they saddled their horses and Rocky explained what he had found. "The pie bald has a rear shoe with a broken-off horn. That will make tracking a bit easier."

The squad waited 15 minutes before heading out of town. They didn't want to risk being spotted. They were banking that Rocky would get them to the camp without losing the track.

Two hours later, Rocky held up and said, "I can smell camp smoke." The horses were ground hitched in a grassy area and started to feed. With moccasins on, Furman was carrying a bag of bear traps, Rocky was still tracking, and the Duos were each carrying long range scoped Win 76's. "This is the plan, Rocky, get us to within 100 yards of camp. Then you and Furman sneak up to their horses and feed them some of this loco weed. That will be the diversion you need to sneak up to the bushes and lay out the bear traps. Once this is done go hide behind some trees, so you don't get accidentally shot from some ricochet. Hannah and I will then take over. As soon as one of the kidnappers goes to the bushes, he'll likely get caught in a trap and will be screaming bloody murder. We'll then shoot and kill some kidnappers. When you hear some giving up, step up and place them in manacles. Now, you need to realize that any plan can go accordingly, or have many variations. If you have to; adapt as is necessary. Good luck and stay safe at all costs."

For the next hour, the duos watched the camp holding their rifles on cross-sticks. The first sign of success is when the outlaw horses were raising a ruckus with loud whinnies and nickers. All four outlaws went to see to the horses. They looked puzzled when all four were acting up. It was assumed that they had eaten some bad grass and simply moved them further from camp. Upon their return to camp, one outlaw walked out heading to the bushes.

Knowing that things would get hot really quick, Jake said, "as soon as you hear the bear trap snap or the outlaw start screaming, the other three outlaws will jump up. At that moment, put one outlaw down and I'll do the same. Hopefully, the last one will surrender, but don't let him trick you, if he points his gun at the victim, put him down immediately."

As expected, the scream came, all the outlaws jumped up. Two loud rifle shots were heard, and two outlaws were knocked down. The third realized that he was next and yelled out that he surrendered. Jake took his eyes off the outlaw, realizing that he had made a terrible mistake. By the time he got his eyes back in the scope, he saw the outlaw's pistol pointing at the victim. Before he could fire, he saw the outlaw's head disappear as Hannah hit him smack in the face. Jake sat there in silence as he finally said, "you were right when you asked to join the squad, you just saved my butt and that young man's life, good work 'chee-kee.'"

"That's ok, hubby. I expect proper thanks tonight, heh?"

The Duo stepped up to the camp and greeted Dempsey. They cut his bindings as he said, "boy I thought I was 'a gonna' when he pointed his pistol at me. I jumped when his face disappeared. Who made that shot anyways?"

When he stood up, he asked, "why is that other one still screaming?"

"You won't believe this, but that 'girl' made that shot." "Well, thank you Ma'am."

"Let's walk over and see our screamer." As they arrived, the outlaw was sitting on the ground and Furman was trying to open the bear trap. Rocky was laughing at Furman's futile attempt that only made the outlaw scream even more. Eventually, with extra help, they got the outlaw out. The top of his boot had been lopped off and he had teeth marks all over his lower leg. Jake poured carbolic acid over the lacerations saying, "we wouldn't want you to get an infection before you hang, would we!"

The boys then released the remaining traps, searched the outlaws' pockets and collected $671 which they distributed evenly. Jake then asked the living outlaw where their stash from previous kidnappings was hidden. The outlaw responded, "you can kill me, 'it don't matter,' since I'm a dead man anyways."

Dempsey said, "let me at him, I'll make him talk."

"No. we don't torture to leave evidence of inhumane treatment. This will make him talk without physical evidence. Jake straddled the outlaw and shove his awl up the root of a rotten molar. Rocky and Hannah had never seen the result and backed up in shock as the outlaw squealed, stiffened up and soiled himself. When Jake pulled the awl, he asked him, "you have several juicy molars, you want another poke?"

"Rotten tree with a hole three feet off ground. There's a tin with the dough. Just keep that thing away from me." Furman was the one who took off to find the stash. Rocky was still laughing but finally said, "I would never have thought that Marshal work could be so entertaining!" Hannah was seen holding both her hands over her mouth but finally uttered, "Jake Harrison, you could have told me about that tool during your presentation the other day. Really!"

"Part of being on the squad, baby—with a grin from ear to ear."

Furman came back with a bundle of money that amounted to $17,500. They then closed camp, loaded the dead outlaws and the near amputee, and headed back to town.

Arriving at Sheriff Bixby's office. They left the bodies for the undertaker, threw the kidnapper in jail and the sheriff said he would check to see how much reward was offered for this gang. Furman then took the outlaw horses to Werner's livery to sell them as well as bringing the outlaw guns to Blackwell's shop for the same purpose. When he came back to the sheriff's office, he gave Jake $320 for the horses and $260 for the firearms. Jake gave the sheriff $100 to pay for the outlaw's housing till the trial.

Finally, the squad with their prize, headed to the railroad hotel. The Peabodys were sitting on the porch and spotted their son from afar. Both Dutton and Isabella were running in the street to reach their son. The meeting was a great show of true love. The squad stepped down from their horses and Jake introduced Rocky and Furman to some very grateful crying parents.

That night, the Duo took a room in the same hotel. Hannah was in the bathtub and

Jake was watching her. When she got out of the tub to dry off, Jake was now staring at her. "Well mister, are you enjoying the view, chee-kee?" "Yes, I like to see you standing 'akimbo' with your hands on your hips, your legs spread apart and your female attributes 'au naturel!" Well, nothing else was said till morning.

At a replenishing breakfast, Dutton came over and sat at the Duo's table. "I owe you more than gratitude," as he pulled out his bank book. Hannah placed a hand on the bank book and said, "instead of that, maybe you can recommend an oil driller. Jake is seriously thinking of digging an oil well on our land."

"Hell, I can do better than that. My brothers are both in the oil business. One is an oil driller and the other is a facilitator of crude oil from storage to refineries. Do nothing and I'll get back to you within a week—and that is a promise. Thanks again."

Before leaving town, the $17,500 was placed in Judge Hobart's account to disburse to the victim's families in Colorado. The rewards amounted to $6,000 which Jake distributed amongst the six squad members. Jake pointed out that although Willie and Walt were in San Antonio on assignment, they would still benefit from the reward money.

As they were saddling their horses, Dutton and Dempsey walked in the livery. Dutton said, "my son doesn't want to return to Denver. He wants to return to cowpunching. I know you have a large ranch outside of town, would you happen to know if you have any openings for new workers?"

"Hey, we always have room for experienced cowhands. Would you be interested in joining my crew?" "Yes sir, I would be honored to work for you." "Ok, then saddle up and join us since we're heading home right now."

"Again, I owe you. His mother will finally be at peace knowing her son is working for the man who saved his life. Now, I just realized that you not only saved my son's life, but you also saved my wife as well. That lady was dying of worry. You'll hear from me in a week. Thanks."

***

CHAPTER 4

TRIBULATIONS AND SPECULATIONS

Arriving at the ranch, Jake spoke to Clayton about the situation with Dempsey. Clayton met with him and was more than happy to add him to the cattle crew.

That evening, after supper, a package arrived for Hannah. Opening the box, she found a package of carbon paper with special erasers. Jake said, "what is this and what is it used for?"

"This is carbon paper. It's made of soot mixed with a special wax. It's placed behind the paper being typed and in front of a second sheet of paper. When the typed letter hits the first sheet, the impact on the carbon paper adds that waxy soot to the second sheet."

"Why is that important?"

"The instructor feels that any book typed must have a copy. Either handwritten or carbon copy. The obvious reason is to guarantee, that if the US Postal Service loses the typed version, the carbon copy can be sent to the publisher to be set to type."

"Humm, good idea. So now, how do you correct typos?"

"After a fully typed sheet is done, you remove both from the typewriter. The typed sheet is corrected by erasing the typos and reinserting the sheet in the machine. After aligning the letters in the vertical/horizontal, you simply retype the correct letter. Now, the carbon paper typos are different. There is this special 'gummy' eraser that removes the waxy soot. Then you have to handwrite the corrected letter with this special pen with black ink. Afterall, the carbon copy is just that, a copy."

"Now, I know why you haven't started

to write. You were waiting for this carbon paper, heh?"

"Correct. Now I have to write my first three to six pages before the class next Wednesday. At our last class, we learned how to prepare an outline before typing away. I have my entire first chapter prepared in this outline, and I will start writing tomorrow. Let's step in my office and I'll demonstrate the entire process."

***

The next morning, during their replenishing breakfast, Tommy arrived with an urgent telegram:

FROM JUDGE HOBART STOP
SAN ANTONIO STOP
UNABLE TO FIND AN UNBIASED JURY STOP
EVERYONE FEELS THE RUSTLERS ARE GUILTY
AND WANT THEM HUNG STOP
DEFENSE REQUESTS A CHANGE OF VENUE STOP

REQUEST ASSISTANCE TO TRANSPORT SUSPECTS BACK TO NEW BRAUNFELS rsvp STOP

Jake wrote his response "On our way today on noon train," and gave Tommy the message to send urgently. Jake then asked Hannah if she wanted to join him and Furman on the prisoner transfer. Hannah said, "it sounds to me that this kind of work is without much of a challenge. If you are comfortable in handling the transfer with three men, then I would prefer to stay home and start writing my pre-class assignment."

"Ok, but you need protection. Remember that Dieter is not a happy puppy with us, and Grant Galvin is being released soon."

"Well, your dad will willingly spend the days roaming about the house, and there is always Rocky who is in the barn when all the crews are out in the crop fields or the cattle range. At night, I'll move into your parents' house. Besides, I always wear my Bulldog. Ok?"

"I guess that is secure enough. See you tomorrow night."

Jake and Furman took the noon train to San Antonio and arrived in an hour. Judge Hobart had arranged for a special express car to be added behind a freight car. This special car had a full jail with iron bars and a massive safe for money transfers between banks and mines. Payrolls were no longer sent by stagecoaches since the railroad had a much better security system and track-record.

Judge Hobart went into detail, "I'll be in the passenger car with a lawyer. This man is the assistant prosecutor in San Antonio, and he may want to move to New Braunfels to be the head prosecutor. He would serve us well from my observations and his name is Cain Bishop. You'll be in the express car with the prisoners and over $10,000 of Wells Fargo money coming to our Ranchers' Bank in town, to cover payrolls for many ranches. Just so you know, the express boxcar locks from the inside and there is a locked escape hatch in the roof of the car for your use if needed. Your horses will be in the stock car as usual."

The train was rolling along by 6AM and if everything went well was expected to be in New Braunfels by 7:30AM. Forty-five minutes in the trip, the train's speed was slowing down. Eventually it was moving at a crawl speed of 5mph. Willie was sent thru the hatch door to go see what the trouble was.

Willie was running faster than the train was moving. When he got to the engine he asked the engineer, "what is the problem?"

"Have a release valve stuck open and I cannot maintain any pressure. We'll be continuing at 5mph for the next three hours to get to New Braunfels."

Just as Willie was about to go back to the express car, the fireman, who was watching the rail, yelled STOP. "There is a rail pulled off ahead." The engineer reacted instantly to the word 'stop' by stepping off the 'dead-man' pedal and all the wheels locked up in a matter of seconds. As Willie was looking at the track, he realized that the rail had been pulled off intentionally. He then said, "get ready, we're going to be attacked and robbed."

At the same time, Furman, Walt and Jake had sneaked up the hatch to see what was going on. Sitting on the express car's roof, they saw a large gang approaching the train from east and west of the track. The gang saw them on the roof and started shooting at them. The squad started shooting back and lead was flying everywhere. The eight gang members had no chance of winning this unexpected surprise. They were moving about on horses and shooting pistols, compared to sitting on the roof shooting rifles. In a matter of minutes all eight gang members were on thc ground and Willie was running towards them to secure the wounded.

The three wounded would survive and were thrown in the barred cell of the express. The five dead ones were thrown in the freight car and their horses were added to the stock car. The engineer then told Willie that someone needed to go a mile to Northcliff where there was a telegraph sub-station and notify the railroad that a repair crew was needed to replace the rail before they could move on.

Willie related the situations and Jake said, “I’m going. Even with a crew on its way, it’s going to be hours before this train arrives in town. I don’t want to leave Hannah any longer than I have to. So, after I relay the message, I’ll continue to cover the nine miles to town and head immediately home. You boys have the situation under control, and I doubt you’ll have more outlaws to deal with.”

Jake relayed the message in Northcliff and then rode toward home. Jake had a strange premonition that something was wrong. All he could do was push his horse to cover the mileage and stop at Sheriff Bixby’s office on the way home.

***

Meanwhile at the ranch, Amos was sitting in the parlor reading the local paper and Hannah was furiously typing away. The words had easily come and she was already on page eight with very few typos. It was 10AM when five riders arrived at the access road. They tied off their horses and started walking towards the Harrison ranch with one horse in tow for a quick return to their other horses. Quietly, they stepped on the porch and entered the unlocked front door. They found Amos asleep and nudged him awake. One man slammed the butt of his pistol on his head and knocked him out.

Hannah had heard a strange noise and called out. "Amos is everything alright?" Amos didn't answer, so Hannah drew her five shot Bulldog. Without warning, men started entering her office with drawn pistols. Hannah never hesitated, she started firing and men were dropping. One man had to be shot twice because Hannah's first shot had hit the man in the shoulder. There in front of her were four men on the floor. Hannah started walking to verify they were dead but in the heat of the moment forgot to reload her pistol. As she was walking amongst the bodies, she felt a sharp pain in the back of her head and then everything went black.

Rocky thought he heard some shooting at the main house and sent Red Flower to check things out. When she returned on a dead run, Rocky simply saddled his horse, took his rifle and went straight to the main house. Making sure that Amos was awakening, Red Flower sent Rocky onward saying, "I'll send the cook to get Sheriff Bixby and I'll go get Clayton and some men. You need to track Hannah's abductor before the sheriff or Clayton arrives. Once you know where the outlaw is hiding, come back here for some help."

The outlaw had Hannah draped in front of himself on the saddle. He made a quick trip to Klaus' ranch. When Dieter saw the idiot regulator arrive with Hannah, he yelled, "get out of here, take her deep in the forest to the south, off my land, and offer Jake the two papers I gave you. Now get and wait for Jake even if it takes days! Since only you survived, get that paper signed and it's worth $1,000 to you."

***

Jake arrived in town and stopped at the sheriff's office, but no one was in the office. Jake stopped a man on the street and found out that Sheriff Bixby had been summoned by a cook and rushed out of town at a full gallop. Jake now knew that something was drastically wrong at the ranch.

Arriving home, Jake recognized Herb's grey horse and rushed in the house. Amos was being attended by Erna and Red Flower. Jake spotted the four bodies who were being searched by Herb Bixby. Herb said, "one body had been shot twice and none of the bodies have any ID's. Jake then remembered how Hannah had asked for a six-shot revolver, but Jake had failed to get her one. Jake then realized that it was likely the fifth outlaw had knocked Hannah out, since there was no evidence of any struggle.

Jake then asked Amos, "can you tell me what happened?" "No, they jumped me and knocked me out."

Red Flower spoke up, "Rocky went tracking the kidnapper. He took off east of here and was to return here as soon as he found the outlaw camp. Head out east while tracking the fresh tracks and hopefully you'll come up on Rocky."

Thank you, Red Flower. Herb, care to join me to get this scoundrel?"

"Right with you Jake, let's go."

"Let me grab my scoped Win 76/cross-sticks and we're off."

***

Herb and Jake were on their way east at a full gallop. The tracks led to Klaus's ranch, but Rocky showed up from the south. "Boss, I found the pig's camp and there are two papers tacked to a tree about 100 yards from his camp. Follow me to that tree." The three took off at a gallop since Rocky knew the way.

Meanwhile, at the kidnapper's camp, he said to Hannah, "take your clothes off, your husband will be here soon, and I want him to see you a bit indisposed."

I'll take my blouse and riding pants off, but I'm not taking off my chemise or underpants. I'm warning you, if you strip these off me, I'll pluck your eyes out. Trust me!"

"Fine, but stand there facing the clearing.

I want him to see me pointing a gun at your head!"

Within a half hour they arrived at the tree Rocky had found. Jake looked at the two papers. They were official quick-claim deeds prepared by the town clerk, Vernon Winston. They were also witnessed by him and the neighboring local barber, Craig Moulton. One was the transfer from Dieter Klaus of lot 34 and 35—the two sections that were north of the new four homesteads, and south of the new public land he had purchased. Jake kept that one and pocketed it. The other was a land transfer from the Harrisons of lot 27 and 28 which bordered the town. That one got crumbled and also pocketed.

Herb added, "that camp is only 100 yards away, how do you want to proceed?"

As Jake was about to speak, the kidnapper appeared with Hannah and yelled out. "Take the land transfer to you, and sign the land transfer to Klaus. Then I'll let your wife go and that will be it. What do you say?"

Jake said nothing. He placed his cross-sticks

down, and laid his scoped Win 76 in place. Looking in the scope, the outlaw was standing behind Hannah and didn't provide a safe shot. Suddenly, Hannah realized that the outlaw was a few inches shorter than she was. Her next move was a sign to Jake.

There she stood akimbo with her hands on her hips and her legs separated. Jake scoped her underpants and saw the outlaw's crotch appear in his scope. Jake took careful aim and slowly squeezed the trigger. The result was a direct hit to the outlaw's crotch as he flailed his arms out while throwing his pistol away. He simultaneously screamed and collapsed to the ground while holding what was left of his privates.

Jake, Herb and Rocky rushed to Hannah with their pistols drawn. Hannah was busy examining herself thru the torn-off crotch of her underpants as she said, "Hubby, that was way too close. You tore off my underpants' crotch, and singed my hairs. Heck, you almost took my 'love button' off. You're going to have to do some more practice with that rifle of yours."

"Stop examining yourself, you're revealing too much of your private business end and your boobs are falling out of your chemise. As Rocky appeared with her blouse and riding pants, Hannah quickly dressed. Rocky turned to the outlaw, took his knife out carved out a piece of each ears and then snipped the end of the outlaw's nose.

The outlaw let go of his crotch as he tried to protect his face from the Indian. Rocky then added, "there you go boss, now he looks like the pig that he really is."

The Duo was not paying attention to the screaming outlaw. Jake had Hannah in his arms and said, "you're a bright lady to stand akimbo, and that shot was placed right where I wanted it. How did you end up being kidnapped after killing four of the abductors?" "Well, I made an error, instead of reloading my Bulldog, I went to check if any of the outlaws were still alive—nerves, I guess. There must have been this one standing behind the doorway because I felt a pain in my head, and then everything went black."

Meanwhile, Herb and Rocky were watching the outlaw bleeding out. He had massive damage to his lower pelvis and his privates had been blown off. When the outlaw realized he was dying, he admitted that Dieter Klaus had paid his gang of regulators to stage the kidnapping in the hopes of forcing Jake to sign the quick-claim deed for lots 27 and 28."

After the outlaw had taken his last breath, he was loaded on his horse. Jake then said, "we're going to see Klaus and bring this pig to him. Then Klaus and I will have a private talk while you wait outside."

Arriving at the Circle K ranch, Jake crashed thru the front door.

Klaus was standing in his parlor looking the flamboyant popinjay he was. Fastidiously dressed in a well-tailored suit, he looked like a puffed- up cockerel. Dieter snobbishly said, "how dare you, entering my home without being invited in?" Without any warning, Herb and Rocky dropped the piggish looking outlaw onto his parlor rug. Dieter changed his denigrating facial appearance to the look of shock and fear.

After Herb and Rocky stepped outside, Jake said, "when I finish trouncing you, you're going to look just like this hog you sent to kidnap Hannah and extort that land you wanted. Jake grabbed Klaus by the shirt collar and lambasted his face with several round punches to his face. His nose was broken and most of his front teeth came flying out. Jake was in a rage and Hannah finally said, let's mark him like the outlaw and that will be enough. Jake pulled out a knife as Klaus declared, "no no nooh! Let's talk this thru and come to a mutual agreement. I can't look like him!"

Jake finally gave Klaus an alternative. "I can arrest you for kidnapping and you'll get a long prison term while the county seizes your land. Or, you can permanently leave this area and file for bankruptcy. You already signed the quick-claim deed to section 34 and 35 and that will be restitution for kidnapping Hannah."

As Klaus was contemplating his choices, Hannah took a more realistic approach and said, "either way you're going to lose your land, it only matters whether you spend twenty years in prison and get raped repeatedly, or you walk away a free man. Make up your mind since Sheriff Bixby is waiting to bring you to jail, heh!"

Dieter Klaus' face changed to the look of resignation. "I guess I was never happy here, even when my adoptive parents were alive. It seems that no one out West could accept my personal and sexual habits, and I'll likely move to the East where alternative lifestyles are more accepted. I'll file for bankruptcy and let the courts dispense the assets to pay for my failed oil drilling expenses and other credits. Besides, the well drilling team is already loading their equipment and will be leaving in the next few days. So, I'm broke and will leave with my personal belongings and a small amount of cash. As for owing you more than those two lots I signed away, you'll be able to buy this entire homestead and its six sections for pennies on the dollar. So, I'm sorry, this was all a mistake on my part. You'll never hear from me again!"

***

The next week, things were quiet for the Harrisons. Judge Hobart was holding court in town on three cases—the rustling in San Antonio, the local Peabody kidnapping and the train robbery attempt. The squad was busy organizing and guarding the trials, and Jake was present only on days he had to testify. During those days, the Duo used their time in town to run errands. They went to see Vernon Winston at the town clerk's office and had an official new deed prepared in both their names to cover lots 34 and 35. They also went to see Judge Hobart's secretary, Hollis Bradshaw, to enquire about the Klaus bankruptcy. Hollis said, "the bankruptcy application has been filed by a local attorney. The assets vs. debts are now being established to determine what percent of assets the creditors will be awarded. Do you have to file a claim against the estate?"

"No, we want to be listed as potential buyers of the six sections of land plus all buildings and equipment—or, the entire homestead."

"I will list you as potential buyers and you'll

be notified when the bankruptcy auction will be held."

The other errand was a long telegram to Nathaniel Duseldorf in Chicago. Requesting a response when possible.

Three days later after testifying in the Peabody kidnapping case, Ted was waiting outside the courtroom with a folder holding several sheets of paper. He told Jake, "This is an official railroad letter of 250 words. This is not allowed by Western Union because it ties up the telegraph for at least a half hour. However, this was authorized by some 'higher-up' on the railroad food chain. Also, this is without doubt the longest telegram I ever transcribed; and we can't charge for it because of who and where it came from. Interesting, heh? I know you'll like the answer enclosed."

They both read the letter and Hannah said, "I knew I shouldn't doubt you, but this request was so outlandish and unrealistic that, well I stand corrected. Where do we go with this, now?"

"We go order a portable steam powered

conveyor belt to transfer hay bales from our two sheds to boxcars. Then we go home and have a meeting with Clayton."

The meeting would wait till after a nice dinner at Natalie's Diner. While waiting for their order, they saw Walt enter the diner and was escorted to a private table. Hannah said, "did you see Natalie welcome Walt with a smile and more than a cordial peck on the cheek."

"Of course, why not? Natalie is a very beautiful woman."

"And how beautiful is she to you?"

"No one could ever match you when you stand akimbo in your birthday suit, dear!" Thankfully, Natalie arrived with their order and then went to sit at Walt's table. Hannah added, "look at that, they're holding hands. Looks like a wedding is in the making, heh?"

***

That afternoon the duo had a business meeting with Clayton. Jake started, "how is winter affecting our hay supply?"

"It's been a cold winter, but we have very

little snow. We have been supplementing the pregnant cows with or without calves, but the other animals can find enough frozen forage to maintain themselves. So, we may only use 10% of our massive inventory in two sheds."

"And what is this inventory in bales or tons?"

"We harvested 300 acres of hay land in two crops. Each acre yielded two tons per acre, or a total of 600 tons in two crops. We also harvested 100 acres of oats and ended up with 100 tons of straw and 35 twenty five pound bags of oats for feed."

"What is this worth in dollars?"

"Locally with a low snow winter, there is no demand so the price per ton is down to $11 a ton—which is the high rate for 1890, six years ago. Now, the northern Texas area between Dallas and Amarillo is being blasted with several feet of snow and there is a high demand for feed which has pushed the value to $20 per ton for hay, $25 per ton for alfalfa, $10 per ton for straw and $10 for a 25 lb. bag of oats."

"So, you're saying that my 600 tons of hay at

$20 a ton is worth $12,000, the straw is worth $1,000 and the oats is worth $350 in Dallas?"

"Yes, and that's the problem, Dallas is 250 miles away."

"Well, for the first time, I'm ahead of you on this. So, we have two issues: shipping hay and finding wholesale customers in Dallas. For the last issue, we need to sign up some customers in Dallas to buy our product. It sounds like we need some Feed and Grain stores to handle feed for city folks who have horses, and we need feed distributors to get hay to ranches north of Dallas to include Amarillo, Lubbock and even Oklahoma City."

"Yes, that is the first problem to resolve."

Hannah asked, "Clayton, you got married two weeks ago, did you go on a honeymoon?"

"No, with all the activity on the ranch, building fences, cultivating new land, moving into our first home, and Sandra wanting to start working on the cultivation project; we decided to put it off till things settled down."

"Oh, 'bull-ticky,' things won't ever settle down, there will always be a new issue to get under control. How would you and Sandra like to go on a fully paid honeymoon to Dallas? It will include train passage, hotels, meals, entertainment and $50 for miscellaneous expenses. It will finish when you find us at least six Feed and Grain stores as well as two or more wholesale distributors."

"Wow, work and play. I accept, I know Sandra will be ecstatic. That is very generous, thank you."

"No, you're doing us a big favor. We assume that your new crop and cattle foremen can hold the fort while you're gone?"

"Yes, they are very capable and conscientious men that you can trust."

"Great, now for the shipping problem. A week ago, I sent a telegram to a high-ranking railroad executive in Chicago. This is a man who was carrying a large railroad payroll during a train robbery. The outlaw was about to shoot him when I shot the outlaw dead as he stood over Mr. Duseldorf. The telegram was to request a side rail from the main trunk-line that passes only a quarter of a mile south of the ranch. This is the telegraph letter I received today, read it yourself."

From: Nathaniel Duseldorf, vice president of development
Railroad Headquarters
Chicago, Illinois

Dear Jake,

It was a pleasure to hear from you, but I admit it rekindled some of my fears from that day when you saved my life. To get to the matter at hand, the railroad will be happy to build you a side rail to your ranch. I have sent my yard engineer to check out your access to the trunk-line and he reports that you are a quarter mile away on flat prairie land. It will include a road traversing bridge to accommodate wagons and horses over the track. The side rail will hold four standard box cars. The new rail cost on flat prairie land is $16,000 *per mile. Your quarter mile would normally cost $4,000 but your recent aborted train robbery when outlaws tried to derail a train has saved the company incredible grief and your cost will be deducted down to $2,000.*

In addition, seeing that we will be getting the freight for your hay, we are charging you $15 per boxcar full of hay to Dallas as long as your men fill four boxcars at one time, and the buyers pick up their own orders—saving us manhours.

I trust this is acceptable. With your request to start, I can have the rails, railroad ties and a work team in your town within three days. Just arrange for your local freight company to be available to start hauling the supplies to the work site. The job will take a week to completion.

My sincere regards--Nathaniel Duseldorf, Executive VP

"Oh my, my hat is off to you. You are proving to be a shrewd and astute businessman. I guess, I only have two questions. If the boxcars are on rails between the barn lean-to shed and the new separate shed, how do we get the bales loaded across the space between the boxcar and the sheds. And how many bales can we get in a boxcar?"

"For loading the bales, I have ordered a portable conveyor—a steam powered belt conveyor that can be used in either shed. This will be here in a few days."

"Now a standard boxcar is roughly 50X10X10 feet or +-5,000 cubic feet. A 50 lb. bale of hay is about 5 cubic feet and at 50 lbs. per bale, it takes 40 bales to make a ton. Well 40 bales occupy 200 cubic feet (40X5). So, 5,000 cubic feet will hold 25 tons of hay (5,000÷200). Now, for your answer, 25 tons of hay equal 1,000 bales per boxcar and at 50 cents per bale, each boxcar is worth $500."

"To further extrapolate, since each boxcar holds 25 tons, then each caravan holds 100 tons, or worth $2,000. Since you claimed that we had 600 tons of hay and 100 tons of straw, then seven caravans will ship all of this year's supply. And next year, we'll have another 100 acres cultivated or maybe more if we buy extra implements and hire more men. There is money to be made if the marketing works well this year."

"To close the matter, let's go over the conditions of sale to either a store or a distributor:

1. Shipment minimum is a half boxcar, or 12.5 tons=500 bales.
2. There are no maximum orders once each contracted customer has received his guaranteed minimum of one box car. The exception being if one customer declines his guaranteed minimum order.
3. Orders only accepted by telegram. Payment with Western Union voucher to accompany order at $20 per ton for hay, $10 per ton for straw and oats at $10 per 25 lb. bag of oats.
4. Buyers pick up their own orders at the railroad yards.

5. Orders are 'first come first served.' When the supply is gone, that's the termination of our contract."

"Very good, start packing for your trip. By the time you return, the side rail will be ready, and I'll have taken delivery of the conveyor belt. If you come back with payment vouchers, we'll be ready to load the first caravan of 4,000 bales."

As the days went by, the rail line was installed, and the conveyor was put together by the crop foreman. At the week's end, a message arrived from Judge Hobart and a telegram was delivered from Dutton Peabody. The request to meet with the judge was as expected, but the news from Commandant Peabody would affect their future forever.

***

CHAPTER 5

OIL-HAY-LAND-CAPERS

Judge Hobart's message was a request to meet in the near future. Dutton's telegram was a bit of a surprise. He basically asked, if someone could meet his two brothers, Emerson and Hayden, at noon today, at the railroad yard. They will have their own horses but need directions to our ranch.

The Duo decided to be at the train themselves and invite them to Natalie's Diner for dinner. Arriving early, Jake had ordered a new Win model 94 in 30-30 caliber with copper jacket bullets and smokeless powder. He had also ordered some smokeless shotgun shells for use in his new 1897 pump shotguns. Hannah knew nothing about this new gun and this new smokeless powder. So, Jake volunteered what he knew about it.

"This new rifle is a 30 caliber that shoots a bullet at 2,000 fps and has a 200-yard range. This copper jacket bullet does not lead the barrel and the powder is non fouling so we don't need to clean the barrel after a shooting session. Because the ammo is almost twice the length of a 44, the magazine only holds five rounds and one in the chamber. The advantage is that in a rifle gunfight, this rifle has twice the range of a Win 73 and will put outlaws at a disadvantage. It is not a replacement for the 400-yard rifle of the scoped Win 76. As for the advantage of smokeless shotgun shells, the new pump has harder steel like the Win 94 and can handle higher pressures without the smoke of black powder. This is an advantage in a face to face gunfight."

"This is all good news, and I'm going to include this in my book since it is the consistent with the times of my story."

After picking up his new gun, they had the time and went to the gunsmith's range to try the rifle out, as well as the new shotgun shells. Hannah commented, "this rifle is very sleek and will fit in the horse's scabbard. There is more recoil but less than the long-range Win 76. I really like it, let's order another for me, heh?" "Of course, dear!"

As the train arrived, the Duo spotted the two dandies with city clothes and derby hats. Introductions were made and the Peabodys were glad to get a home cooked meal after traveling 900 miles over 30 hours. The first thing they ordered was a 16-ounce steak with plenty of coffee. Waiting for their meal over two pots of coffee, the Peabody brothers explained what they were planning.

Hayden started, "we are here to dig you an oil well and provide a delivery system to the railroad. We have been hired by our wealthy brother, Dutton, to do this as thanks for saving our nephew—who we are looking forward to see since he now works for you, heh."

Emmerson took over, "do you know where

you have surface seepage and is there any experience in drilling anywhere close to you?"

Jake said, "our neighbor dug three wells. The driller had a rig that was limited to 1,300 feet. The first well at six miles east of us was dry at 1,300 feet. The second well at four miles east of us was also dry at 1,300 feet. The third well now two miles east of us showed oily chips at 1,300 feet but the well was abandoned since it reached its maximum drilling depth. Our neighbor tried to buy the two sections two miles west of his last dig because their geologist felt our land would produce oil at 1,000 feet. Now this land he wanted to buy is only 400 yards to the railroad yard."

Emmerson said, "do you know what the cost is in drilling 1,300 feet?

"Yes, about $35,000—based on $20 a foot for the first 500 feet and +-$40 a foot thereafter. But we also realize that if we hit oil at a production of 100 barrels per day, at the current rate of $1 per barrel, we could pay for the well in one year. We consider this a good investment."

"Well your estimates are conservative, but it

is closer to $40,000. In any event, I will guess that you're going to hit oil at +-700 feet if he had oily chips two miles east of you. If that's the case, then this well would cost you in the vicinity of $20,000."

Jake pulls out his bank book and starts writing, "would you accept a deposit of $10,000 to get the project started"

Hayden put his hand on Jakes writing hand and said, "sir, you don't understand. This well will cost you nothing. Dutton is paying for everything and he can surely afford it. So, put away your bank book and let's eat," as Natalie arrived with their meal.

After a wonderful dinner, the Peabodys picked up their horses at the stockcar's corral and they headed to the ranch. They walked the two sections of land and Emmerson chose a spot some 100 yards away from the surveyed border. Hayden then taped off the distance to the railroad yard and came up to 425 yards.

Hayden then added, "you are lucky, we'll build a six-inch pipeline in the town's road right-of-way and deliver the crude oil directly at a receiving station in the railroad yard. That way, the oil barrels will be directly loaded onto the rainproof boxcars."

Hannah added, "why such a large pipe, wouldn't a 4-inch pipe do as well?"

"Not if you decide to drill a second or third well. As it is, crude oil is so sludgy that we'll add a pump to push the crude along. Fortunately, the town is downhill which will minimize the pump's workload."

Hayden added, "now we're going back to town. We have to pay your town clerk for the use of the road's right-of-way. We'll stay at the railroad hotel and will receive our equipment on tomorrow's train. Tomorrow we have a dozen men and a cook arriving as well as everything we need to set up a tent city on the drilling site, and the complete set up to drill a water well with a windmill pump. The next day, the oil derrick arrives with 400 oak barrels. The oak barrels will stay stored in two boxcars since each boxcar holds 200 barrels doubly stacked. The third day will bring the pipes and the drill itself. The last train will have the transferring pipes with the pump and receiving station, as well as a steam powered bulldozer for cleanup. We'll arrange everything with the railroad clerk and pay the necessary fees."

The Duo was totally taken back with all the organized deliveries. Hannah finally said, "seems like a massive arrival of supplies, what happens if we don't hit oil?"

Emmerson answered, "Ma'am our drill can go 1,500 feet. Without a doubt, we'll hit oil. See you tomorrow."

Jake added, "I've made arrangements with Bromley Freighting, but you may want to verify that they'll be there to load your supplies."

***

Later that day, the Duo went to have a meeting with Judge Hobart. "It's been a very hectic week with the trials. Your men were very helpful in organizing the entire events and the new prosecutor, Cain Bishop, was well prepared and very professional in delivering clear evidence of the outlaws' guilt. Cain has applied for the prosecutor position and Clifton is willing to resign since he really wants to go in private practice with his wife. So, unless you object, the change will occur effective immediately."

"Sounds good to me."

"Good, now at the trials, all accused were found guilty, half got prison sentences and the others will hang tomorrow. Can you be with your men since this is their first experience as assistants to the hangman?" "Of course, I'll be here with Rocky and Hannah."

"Now, the second matter is about a winter haven for outlaws in Austin. Because of the heavy snow and cold winter in Dallas and Amarillo, outlaws have gathered in Austin. Marshal Gideon Granville has requested help in arresting these outlaw gangs. Presently, he and his deputies are investigating which gang is in their city, where they hang out and where they sleep. Once this information is gathered, your team is requested to assist them in making the arrests."

"We're ready and we'll take the train as soon as that telegram arrives. That brings up a topic that my men asked me, but I didn't know the answer. What constitutes a federal crime and what other conditions justify the assistance of US Marshals and the Federal Court?"

"It's not well established but it starts with events in my jurisdiction which covers Austin to San Antonio. The crimes and events include:

- Kidnapping.
- Bank robbery.
- Crimes on federal land including reservations.
- Crimes across state lines.
- Mail fraud or robbery.
- Counterfitting.
- Abusive sexual acts to include rape.
- Assault, threat, or murder of a lawman or judge.
- Malfeasance.
- Others. This is to include the request for US Marshals' assistance in maintaining law and order. This includes requests from any lawman, local and district judges, and even town officials without resident lawmen."

"As you can see, it is a broad definition. This means, there's plenty of crime to keep us busy. The last category is what allows your team to get involved in helping city Marshal Grandville."

***

The executions were scheduled for the next day. Jake wondered if any of the outlaws scheduled to hang might have friends who could try to free their buddies. So, to be on the safe side, he decided to spend the night in the jail with Walt.

Things were quiet in the jail till 3AM. Jake woke up to the sound of a wagon appearing next to the front door. Four outlaws pulled out a huge tree out of the wagon and all four were preparing to ram it into the steel front door. Jake and Walt were ready with their sawed-off shotguns. As they brought the tree at a full run, Jake opened the door and stood back. The tree's momentum kept moving forward and the tree with its four outlaws went barreling down the front office. In the next seconds, the outlaws drew their guns as the Marshals let go with four shotgun blasts. The outlaws were thrown against the wall and were all dead before they fell to the floor.

Sheriff Bixby was sleeping in his jail and awoke in a startle hearing the shotgun blasts. He grabbed a shotgun and ran to the courthouse jail dressed in his union suit. "What in hell happened here?"

"It appears these four idiots assumed they could overpower us and release their friends." Walt added, "and that's what happens when a plan is put together by galoots working with a brick short of a load!"

'Well let's check them for some ID. They may have rewards on their heads, seeing they might have had a connection with the prisoners going to the gallows."

By 9AM the six outlaws were individually hung without any hitch. All six members, including Hannah, of the Marshal Service were present and assisted the undertaker in moving the bodies to the cemetery. The event had a somber effect on the Marshals, as each one returned to their home. It was two days later that the four breaking-in outlaws were found to have an individual bounty of $500 each.

The next morning, Hannah was busy typing away as soon as a replenishing breakfast was finished. Jake was watching her and said, "do you want me to do your chicken routine today?"

Hannah stopped typing and said, "No, I have made changes. I'm so involved with writing that I asked my friends to take over my chores. Camilla is feeding the chickens and collecting the eggs before she waitresses at Natalie's noon meal. Josie is delivering the eggs on her way to work in her husband's law office. Laura has taken over the garden completely. Sandra does any necessary cultivating in the evenings. Even Natalie is helping out by bringing one full meal each day. And I'm free till we go on Marshal duty or till my book is done."

"This is clearly a larger project than I had envisioned. How far along are you?"

"I'm on page 118 out of a proposed 350-page novel. I just finished the first of four books which will all tie together eventually. Once I start writing, the ideas are rushing in faster than I can type. Each paragraph is an explosive sequence just like wang leather, heh!"

"What is wang leather and how is it explosive?"

"Well, you know that wang leather is made from the penis of a bull." "Yes, so what?"

"Well they use it to make wallets.

"Again, so what and why is it explosive?"

"Because, if you rub it vigorously, IT EXPLODES INTO A SUITCASE—HA, HA, HA, HA, HA. . . . . . .HA, HA!!!!!!

"Funny, very funny." Hannah couldn't stop laughing and finally stood up and said she had to go to the water closet. "I laughed so much that I peed in my pants."

"I thought that was a problem of old women who had given birth?"

"True, but the way you make love lately, sometimes I wonder if you're not trying to kill me with your vigor. As a result, things are getting overstretched down there and holdback is not as good as it was. But I'm not complaining mind you. It's just that the "suitcase" could be a bit smaller!" Jake threw his hat at Hannah and walked to his office with a grin from ear to ear as he mussitated, "*and whose fault is that?*" While Hannah was still laughing all the way to the water closet.

***

Tommy arrived the next morning with a message from Judge Aiken. "Hannah, the bankruptcy auction is this afternoon. We need to go. How much land should we try to buy?"
"I think we should get as much as possible, especially with your expanding the crop enterprise. Plus, I suspect you'll be delaying the sale of new stock once the crossbreeding takes over. We could double and even triple our herd if we were to buy Klaus' six sections"

"That is 3,840 acres. At the current rate of 75 cents an acre for land bordering the town road, plus $500 for the ranch house, bunkhouse and barn, we're talking of +-$3,400. If we can get it at 50 cents an acre, we're talking of +-$2,500 and that would be a bargain."

"On second thought, we need that land and those buildings. Go as high as $1 an acre if the bidding competition is aggressive. We have the money and it's our future we're talking about."

"Ok, Hannah, I agree. Grab the bank book and let's go."

At the courthouse, Hollis Bradshaw, was taking registrations. He explained that there were people who wanted to buy five acre building lots on the town road, several couples who wanted to buy the homestead buildings, and some ranchers who wanted to buy the entire homestead to include land and buildings. His last bit of information was that this was a cash sale in order to be a bidder. The Duo registered in the last category—going for the entire holdings.

Bidders and spectators filled the courtroom as Judge Aiken started the auction with an explanation, "we are here to sell this property to include land and buildings and all the furnishings and tools in three buildings. We will try to sell the entire package to one buyer. If there are none, then we will start selling lots and buildings piecemeal. If we sell piecemeal, the buyer will pay the surveying fees. As it is, the entire property was surveyed after Hans Klaus demise."

"So, do we have any bidders who are interested in the entire holdings? Three hands went up. Jake said, "those two competitors are adjacent ranches to the east, they will be aggressive bidders."

"That land adjacent to the road is listed at 75 cents an acre. Do we have a first bid?" "I bid 25 cents an acre to include the buildings."

"That's too low, I won't accept such a bid, anybody else?"

The other bidder said "yes, how about 35 cents an acre?"

The first bidder increased it to 40 cents plus the buildings.

Jake then placed his first bid, "50 cents an acre plus buildings"

The first bidder said, "too expensive for me, I'm out."

The second bidder said 55 cents all inclusive. Jake looked at Hannah and smiled as he said 60 cents to include the three buildings.

Judge Aiken looked at the second bidder

who shook his head and added, "not worth it at that price. I'm out!"

"Any new bidders?" The courtroom was silent. Judge Aiken yelled, "going once. . . .going twice. . . . . .SOLD to Jake and Hannah Harrison of the Circle H Ranch for $2,304. With the cash, my secretary Mr. Bradshaw will prepare the deed which you can file with the town clerk today. Congratulations, you and the creditors got a fair deal."

***

Days later, Clayton and Sandra arrived from their business and honeymoon trip to Dallas. Hannah asked Sandra how they enjoyed their trip? Sandra said, "it was a trip of a lifetime. Dallas is a beautiful city, we visited, we ate in great restaurants, we had plenty of private time, we shopped and went to the theater for a comedy. Thank you so much and the dining car/Pullman berths were a very nice touch. This was an event we'll never forget, and we'll be forever grateful to be in your employ."

"Great, and how did the hunt for hay

customers go?" "Well, after the word was out that we had hay for sale, I began to feel like I was the one being hunted. There was a very high demand for hay and straw and a very poor supply. I visited eight feed stores and each one ordered their guaranteed minimum of one boxcar or 25 tons or $500. Then I negotiated with the two distribution centers. They each wanted eight boxcars or 200 tons or $4,000. And of course, they wanted all 200 tons tomorrow. Each customer wanted straw after all the hay was gone. Each day, we were carrying thousands of dollars, so we started a bank account in your ranch's name and made the bank draft deposits nightly. At the end of the selling spree, you had $16,000 which we sent to your town bank, the Ranchers Bank, by wire transfer. I checked on arrival in town and your money got here before we did."

"I can't believe these businesses paid you cash without knowing the quality of the hay and straw."

"Jake, as one distributor said, 'if you were selling baled loco weed or thistle, I'd buy it.'

Ranchers are losing their herds from deep snow just north of Dallas and ranchers are coming from Amarillo with wagons and staying in town till hay comes in by rail. These are desperate times for ranchers, and they need help."

"Can the private feed stores hold out for a couple weeks?"

"Yes, they've been rationing their customers and have a small supply in their warehouse that will last that long."

"Ok, well the siderail is done and there are four boxcars in our yard. I think we need to put every man we have to load the boxcars and start sending hay to the two distributors. They'll each get their 200 tons ASAP."

"In that case, I'll see the yard manager and ask for an engine to pull these four boxcars by tomorrow night, and bring us four more boxcars. And what is new on the home front?"

"We had a bankruptcy auction on the Klaus ranch. We had the winning bid at 60 cents an acre plus all buildings and contents."

"Wow, what a deal. That's about 4,000 acres with good water and fertile land. That will bring your ranch up to 14,000 acres, and allow us to double your herd and expand your crop acreage. That's great, we now have a mega-ranch."

"This recent purchase changes the layout of our fences. This is what we want. Fence the entire north border from west to east. Continue the south border by allowing for crop acreage next to the town road and fence it also west to east. The east and west borders will follow the surveyed lines except for 300 square acres adjacent to town for oil wells."

"Oil wells, that's a new twist. Are our men going to be involved with that?"

"No, that will be a separate entity. For now, let's continue to lay out the posts to enclose our 14,000 acres. Then, when that's done, we'll start laying out the barbwire. I realize that this is a big order especially with the need to ship hay ASAP. We now have a second bunkhouse at the Klaus ranch. Do you think you could find a cook and a dozen men to start a second team of fencers managed by one of your foremen?"

"Heck yes, the entire laid-off Klaus cowpunchers and their cook is still looking for work. I'm sure one of my foremen will take over that team. That's going to require plenty of shovels, post hole diggers, picks, and posts."

"Get the tools at Heinz's Hardware and I've taken care of the posts. There are 3 mills around town and all of them are working only to fill out our order and deliver posts to the work site. Plus, I've ordered two flat cars thru Mr. Heinz and those are scheduled to arrive in two days. Bromley Freight will bring those to the ranches. I have also started to store barbwire in the hay sheds, and will now speed up that process as the hay sheds empty out."

"That's good because the ground is now frozen, and digging has stopped. Fortunately, we had anticipated this and early in the winter we dug holes and planted the posts. That will allow us to start laying wire till the earth thaws out, and keep the new team of men working."

"Ok, I now have my orders, get the hay out and the fence in, heh!" "And I'll make sure the posts and barbwire continue to come in."

***

The next day, the Duo was watching the Peabody brothers at work. They had the water well dug, the windmill pump up, and the derrick half way up. Emerson said, "we'll be drilling in two days." As they were watching, Jake asked Emmerson, "how do you plan to clean up assuming we hit a gusher?"

"There are two new things in well drilling. There is a new method for capping a gusher that minimizes the amount of crude to clean up. Plus, we have a deflector installed that tends to send the oil in one spot that helps to localize the debris. Then our steam powered bulldozer will dig a trench, scrape the crude/soil into the trench, and then bury it."

"So, while the well is capped, Hayden then connects the pipeline and sets up a receiving station in the railroad yard as well as a pump near the well?"

"Yes, and as you can see, he has obtained a permit to lay a pipeline in the town's right of way, and is dropping pipes on the ground fifty yards from the center of the road. These pipe sections will be ready to be connected as soon as we hit oil. In addition, the pump and receiving station have already arrived and stored in the rail yard's warehouse."

That evening, Tommy arrived with a telegram from Marshal Grandville. It appeared that the reconnaissance was done, and their help was needed to make the arrests. Jake got his team ready and all six marshals headed out, by train, for Austin some 50 miles east.

Arriving in the city, the US Marshals went straight to see city Marshal Grandville. "Thank you for helping us out. I'm too old and my deputy is a greenhorn. Our city is infested and has become a winter haven with the worst of outlaws. Although, the saloons, diners, whore houses, and hotels are enjoying the profits, they are also living in the fear that these men are senseless killers and could murder anyone of them anytime. We have already had several rapes, muggings with robbery, and unjustified gunfights with dead local residents. Now, we have identified five gangs that range from four to eight members. We know where they eat, sleep, gamble, drink and which bawdy house they visit. The town fathers want these gangs arrested and shipped out to where their warrants were issued. Yes, they are all wanted—some alive and many dead or alive. I have the bounty rewards all laid out for you."

"Very good, we're staying at the Texas Belle Hotel. Do any of the gangs stay there?" "Yes, the Swift gang, wanted alive for bank robbery in Dallas." "Then we'll start with cleaning the hotel out."

Registering, they took three rooms. When the manager was asked about the Swift gang, he said, "there are five rowdy drunks that arrive every night around midnight. They hoot and holler and we can hear them arriving on the boardwalk. They continue their antics in the hotel lobby and their big thrill is to walk down the hallways and pound on peoples' doors. Often, they shoot their guns in the floor and the entire hotel empties out the next morning. As much as they pay for their stay, in the long run, they make their stay here a losing proposition. I'd do anything to get rid of them."

Jake added, "well you're in luck, we're US

Marshals and we'll arrest this gang tonight. If it's ok, some of us will be waiting in your bar, some in their room, while the others will be pretending to read in your lobby. When the rabble rousers arrive, we'll take them into custody, hopefully without firing a shot."

After supper at a local diner, the squad walked the streets to note where the saloons were located. They were dressed as cowboys without their signature uniform of a hickory shirt, grey pants, charcoal vest and a black hat. Under their vests was their badge. Each Marshal wore his usual preferred side arm. To avoid detection as a lawmen squad, they tended to walk about in sets of two.

Around midnight, Jake and Hannah were reading in the hotel` lobby, the three deputies were in the bar and Rocky was waiting for them in his room. To everyone's surprise, the Swift gang arrived early at 11PM. As they entered, they were clearly drunk, and they hollered guffaws and chortles at the top of their lungs. One outlaw started walking down the hallway banging on doors. As he approached Rocky's room, Rocky yanked his door open and smacked the butt of his rifle in the outlaw's forehead as he dropped like a pole-axed beef.

Suddenly. The remaining four outlaws were surrounded by marshals. "You're under arrest for robbing the Farmer's Bank in Amarillo. Put your hands up, you're not wanted for murder and will be looking at a prison sentence. If anyone goes for his gun, he's going to die, and that is a promise." The outlaws surrendered, their wrists manacled, and were escorted to Marshall Grandville's jail.

The next day, the Brewster gang was spotted in the Rusty Bucket saloon. This was a large gang of eight members who were wanted for marauding the countryside ranches just north of Lubbock. Their depredations included murder, rape and torture. They were wanted dead or alive. The squad went straight to arrest them.

Jake laid out his plans. "Hannah, you get behind the bar and make sure the bartender doesn't grab his shotgun under the bar to enter the fracas. Rocky, you go to the back door and watch the back side of the gang. Walt, you wait on the porch and make sure no one starts shooting at us thru the batwing doors. Furman and Willie will be my backup. Willie you'll stay with your back to the wall so you can see all the patrons who might pull out a gun. Furman, you'll be on my left side and will be my backup with your pump shotgun at the ready. Now remember, there are eight members and will likely be seated at two tables. We'll have to be astute to identify the second table before they start shooting at us. Remember, stay safe even if it means we start shooting to get control of these killers."

Without any questions, the squad prepared to take their assigned positions. Jake looked over the batwing doors and identified the table with Brewster facing the bar. The Trio entered with Hannah following and Rocky at the rear door. Jake walked straight to Brewster's table and said, "we're US Marshals and you're all under arrest. Stand up and put your hands up." They all stood up, but no one put their hands up.

Hannah, who had the bartender under her shotgun, asked him which table held their partners. When the bartender refused to answer, Hannah shoved her shotgun's barrel into the man's gut was as much force she could muster. The man bent over, croaked some noise and finally pointed at the correct table. Hannah yelled, "you three get up and join your boss." Jake looked up and realized that an outlaw was missing and was probably visiting the outhouse.

Things then went downhill fast. Brewster said, "we're all wanted for crimes that will hang us all. So, we're not going to jail without a fight. It's eight of us against the three of you and a woman." At that moment, everyone heard a thud outside followed by a loud grunt as one man had been taken out, as Walt said, "all clear here, boss!" In a moment, another loud grunt was heard as a man from the second table ended up face first on the table with a rock on a stick next to his head. Jake then said, "it looks like you're down two of your sycophants, so it's now six to six, heh?"

Brewster's face turned red and his eyes were squinting. "I'll kill you myself as he went for his gun." Jake never hesitated, he turned his pistol at

Brewster and shot him in the neck. At the same time, a loud shotgun blast was heard as Hannah was holding the smoking gun. Apparently, she saw someone from the second table draw a gun and was about to shoot Furman. Everyone's head turned to find the outlaw holding a pistol while dead on the floor.

Jake then said, "you've got two dead, two knocked out. So, what will it be? A chance to get a prison sentence at trial or dying today." The remaining four outlaws were not headstrong and easily surrendered.

Later that day, Jake asked Rocky what he had used to knock that outlaw down. "It was my father's old war club—a rock the size of a medium apple tied to a wooden handle by rawhide strips. It flies true and I had to use it since shooting the outlaw would have likely hit some innocent patrons. Besides, that was an easy shot for me to make!"

While getting the living ready to go to jail, Willie said that the outlaw on the porch was dead. Walt said, "guess I hit him too hard." So, five outlaws were escorted to jail. It was

Willie's idea to stay with Rocky at the nearby livery. "Some of these outlaws will have heard the shooting at the Rusty Bucket and when they realize that US Marshals were in town, would be high tailing to their horses to get out of town."

Jake agreed and continued on to the jail. Meanwhile, with the hostler's permission, Rocky hid in the grain closet and Willie hid in the tack room. The livery man stayed with the six horses in their stalls. Without warning, the front door busted open and five well healed outlaws holding their saddlebags and rifles rushed inside. "Get our horses saddled, we're leaving now!"

Rocky and Willie came out of hiding. Willie announced, "put your hands up. I'm sure you belong to some outlaw gang and we're taking you in to check the wanted posters." Just as the word were spoken, one outlaw standing behind Rocky's horse was seen going for his gun. Rocky saw him and quickly made a devilish noise. Rocky's horse responded by lifting his butt and kicking with both hoofs. The outlaw caught one shoe in the neck and one on his face. He was thrown across the room and was dead before he fell to the floor. The other outlaws surrendered in the face of two lawmen holding sawed-off shotguns. After the hostler applied wrist manacles, they were also escorted to Grandville's jail.

The next day, after a replenishing breakfast, Jake and Hannah did some shopping as the remainder of the squad was free and would meet at Bubba's Diner for supper. The duo went into a gun shop but came out with nothing in hand. They then entered a clothing store and realized that all these clothes were available at home. They also went to snoop around a bookstore/ typing center but found nothing they didn't already have. The agricultural implement store was a similar story. They had all the modern implements available today. And so went the rest of the day. Hannah finally said, "Jake we have everything we need and want. Let's go to our hotel and enjoy what we really want?"

"Woman, have you no shame. We are

intimate twice a day as it is, and you want one more today?" "Why of course." "Yes, ma'am."

Waiting for their men, the Duo needed an extra replenishing meal, but nothing was hinted when the squad arrived. After placing their orders, Furman asked, "what's our caper tonight?"

"There's a gang of well-off dandies in town that visit Madame Sylvie's House of Pleasure every night. They're from Fort Worth and are a bunch of flimflam card sharks who cheat. When a player finds out they are cheating, he ends up dead. Somehow, they always get off claiming self-defense until a month ago. They got into a gunfight and several patrons were killed, now they are wanted dead or alive by the families of the victims. Their leader is, would you believe, Phineas Pisscann." Hannah said, "did you say Pisscann?" as everyone broke out in guffaws and more chortles. After the laughter stopped, Jake added, "but don't forget, they all have a mini pistol in their hidden shoulder holster, and these are men who have no respect for laws or lawmen. That makes them even more dangerous."

The squad went to the House of Pleasure and were greeted by Madame Sylvie, a rotund woman with massive boobs. "What can I do for you, and women are not allowed in here. Jake spoke, "we are US Marshals and are here to arrest Pisscann and his buddies. Where are they?"

"They are upstairs, but you're not allowed to interrupt their paid-up session. Now sit down and wait." The boys looked at each other and realized they had been dressed down by this dominatrix. Hannah would have none of it and stepped forward as she punched the Madame to the floor. Quickly, she sat on her massive chest, opened her mouth, and shoved Jake's awl deep in a black molar. Madame Sylvie wet herself and squealed like the pig she resembled. After pulling out the awl, Madame Sylvie said "rooms #1, 2, 6 and 8."

As the squad headed upstairs, all four dandies were caught in the act with their pants and shoulder pistols looped over the bed posts.

There was screaming, swearing and threats of bodily harm, as all four arrogant popinjays were manacled and walked to jail in their unbuttoned union suits. During the collection of guns, Jake noticed a six shot 41 caliber mini pistol in double action. He pilfered the pistol and shoulder rig and handed it to Hannah.

"There you go dear; this is what you asked for before you were kidnapped." "Yes dear, I now have that sixth shot which can make the difference. My five shot Bulldog will now permanently be in my reticule."

The next morning, while talking with Marshal Grandville, it became clear that several groups of "Winter Austins" had left town overnight. "We assume that these were 'winter outlaws' who now know you are rounding up their friends, and they elected to leave before being recognized an arrested."

"Well in that case, let's settle up and we're going home." At that moment a loud demand came from outside the office. "Hey Marshals, get out here. We've had it with your rounding up our friends, get out and face us or we're going to shoot-up this town and kill as many town folks as we can."

Jake looked out the window and saw six outlaws. Marshal Grandville said, "that's the Mad-Dog Harris gang. They are real gunfighters with dead or alive wanted posters." Jake naturally said, "Hannah go to the left boardwalk with your pump shotgun and watch the rooftops across the street. Walt and Willie stand on my left with your sawed-off shotguns. Furman and Rocky, do the same on my right. Each man has his own outlaw to put down, I'll take the two in the middle."

The squad stepped outside and warned the face to face outlaws that if they went for their pistols, that they would all die from shotgun blasts full of buckshot. The four marshals were now pointing their shotguns at the outlaws, hoping the impending devastation from close range shotguns would deflate the situation. Such was not to be the case as the squad members saw time come to a stop. Suddenly their leader yelled, "now." The street turned into a cloud of smoke from the 10-gauge black powder shotgun shells. The outlaws were all down as three shotgun blasts were heard—bang, ka-chin, bang, ka-chin, bang, ka-chin—as a man was seen standing on the nearby roof with a rifle in his hands and then tumbled onto the street. Again, Hannah was seen holding her smoking pump shotgun.

The next day, Marshal Grandville again said that more groups left during the night and that the Marshal's job was done. Marshall Grandville had prepared a balance sheet for the final financial settlement.

"28 horses with saddles and tack @$60=$1,680 plus 28 pistols @$30=$840, plus 8 derringers @$20=$160, plus 28 rifles @$45=$1,260, and that comes to $3,940 for Captain Ennis." Jake added, take one mini pistol out and the eight derringers. Hannah gets one pistol and the derringers go to our women back home. Make the changes and Captain Ennis wont object."

The Marshal continued. "There were 28 outlaws captured dead or alive and the total bounties came to $16,000 as he hands Jake with multiple western union vouchers. Jake takes a

$1,000 voucher out and hands it to Marshal Grandville. This is for you and your deputy as well as covering undertaker fees, train transfers to outlying towns for outlaw trials, feeding the prisoners till they are transferred, paying for a jailer to stay in the jail all night, for your hours of early reconnaissance, and taking the time to gather all these vouchers on our behalf."

The squad gathered their belongings while Jake divided up the vouchers into six payments of $2,500. Then they all took the evening train back to New Braunfels. The Duo was eager to see how the fencing was coming along, how deep the drilling had progressed, how the hay transfers had gone, how many new acres were cultivated, how the calving season was going, and Hannah could finally get back to writing.

Jake realized that certain changes needed to be made regarding the egg enterprise, the type of crops to be planted, and the change in castrating bulls to enable Jake's plan.

***

CHAPTER 6

CHANGES AND DELEGATION

As the Duo got home, they saw a note tacked to their front door. Hannah took it, said it was from Sheriff Bixby, and read it. She was a bit surprised and handed it to Jake. He read it out loud, "just to let you know, Grant Galvin was released from jail where he served his 30-day sentence for tax evasion. Also, the second bidder on the Klaus land auction sale was one of Galvin's employees. I suspect he was bidding just to raise the bid to make you pay more for the land than it should have been valued on a bankruptcy auction. Watch out, the word from prison is that he's going to get some payback once out. Signed, Herb."

Jake said, "Anytime a man in power is humiliated, revenge is a guarantee in the near or distant future. So, we wear a pistol at all times, including church, the chicken coop or even our bedroom. Plus, I've ordered four large bells on pedestals with large steel ringers. If we need help from our bunkhouse, Clayton, Willie, Cliftons or Belchers, all we have to do is ring the bell. I plan to use the bell system if I need Willie and Furman for an emergency marshal response. But it will also be used if we need emergency help from anybody, including my dad."

"Well, I'm happy with that. Let's have supper and then meet with the Peabodys. It seems that our activities this next week will be centered around the drilling." "Ok, but I'll leave a message with the cook that I want to meet with Clayton tomorrow after breakfast. We have much to discuss, and let's hope we don't get a 'call to arms' from Herb or one of the judges!" Emerson was pleased to announce that they were drilling in soft to medium hard rock and had reached 600 feet. The chips were still without an oily covering but the water cleaning the chips out was getting cloudy and something was expected within another 100 feet. Emerson added, "we hope you'll be around for the next week when we expect things to be very active." "Yes, we have many plans to work out and we'll both be in our office till you call for us."

That evening, the Duo enjoyed some quiet time. Jake had a subject to discuss with Hannah and slowly started, "Hannah, don't you think it is time to make changes to the egg business. We now have 20 employees on this ranch and 12 on the other ranch, and each of these men eat four to six eggs for breakfast with 2-4 bangers. I think it is time to reduce our chicken population on this ranch to 125 birds, and keep the eggs to feed our men. Plus, we transfer 100 birds to the Klaus ranch also to feed the men. Each of the ranch's cooks will now be responsible for picking up the eggs and feeding the layers. The Bauer ranch can be expanded to 300 birds since the Newmann's have plenty of help from a paid worker-neighbor called Yvonne Washington. What do you think?"

Hannah was pondering as she exclaimed, "do we know that name, Washington?"

"It seems so, but I can't place it for now."

"Anyways, of course you're a right. It is time I let go of the chicken responsibility. The Newmann's will run the commercial side, and the cooks and their helpers can take care of the coops, chickens and eggs. I want to continue the Marshal assignments, and I want to take over the business books. You have enough to do planning changes for the cattle, crops and now likely the oil business. Besides, I need to be involved with this massive ranch business affairs. I want to know what things cost, where the money is going, and where the profits are. Along with all this, I will also be freer to work on my book."

"Wow, that was a lot easier than I anticipated. Why?"

"Why not, it only makes sense. Besides, as my husband, I know you have my best interest at heart and are usually on top of things. No pun intended, but now it's time for bed etcetera, etcetera and etcetera."

"Speaking of being on top of things, are you going to rub my wallet? No pun intended, heh."

"Until the seams break, for sure!"

The next morning, after a replenishing breakfast, Clayton showed up, this time with a clipboard and a long list of items to discuss. "Boy, I'm glad your back, we need to make decisions."

"If I wasn't back, what would you have done?"

"I would have made them on my own, but when you're here, it's nice to discuss the options." "I agree, I have many things to bring up, but let's start with items from your list."

"First, castration. Spring calving is about to begin, and we need to agree on a plan. Is it the same as our initial plan months ago?"

"No. I am planning a show next fall when the calves are six months old. First, castrate all the pure line Texas Longhorn bulls. We don't want them breeding our cattle. We'll use them to compare with crossbreed steers. Then, I need six steers of pure Hereford, six of pure short horns, and a dozen steers of crossbreeds with Herefords and a dozen of crossbreeds with short horns. All other bulls are not to be castrated. The purebreed and crossbreed bulls will be for sale next spring to start crossbreeding programs with the neighbors."

"Perfect, now what about burning horn buds."

"I've changed my mind on that one. I'm trying to convert my herd to a polled herd. Spring branding is the perfect time to burn horn buds and be done with it. So, every calf's horn buds get zapped off."

"Now how's the fencing coming along."

"We've wired all the posts that were planted before the ground froze. We're already digging post holes but that will slow down when the calving season starts since the cowboys will be roaming the pastures looking for cows with birthing problems. The new team at the second ranch will continue fencing till the project is done."

"How did the hay and straw deliveries go?"

"The conveyor belt was a godsend. There were no railroad glitches, and you have ten 'thank you telegrams' for the high quality you delivered and a fair price. The two distributors also sent you a deposit of $1,000 each toward next year's order."

Clayton then added, "and that brings us to cultivated lands. With late ground freezing and little snow, we were able to cultivate most of the winter. We now have 200 acres of new ground ready for planting plus last fall's 100 acres of oats and the original 300 acres for a total of 600 acres. Five hundred acres should yield 1,000 tons of hay and another 100 acres should yield 200 tons or more of alfalfa as originally planned. And let's plan on cultivating 100 acres of new oats for a mid- summer planting. Hannah will send out contracts this summer, and by the way, she will now be the new accountant and office manager. On this subject, are we going to need more hay storage sheds?"

"No, we're going to have the boxcars handy and will be loading some bales directly off the baler platform with the use of the conveyor belt.

We are going to need to duplicate our harvesting implements. We'll need three mowers, three balers, two each of side rake, finish rake, loader, tedder, and hay wagons. I have already ordered these as well as six more work horses. Finally, remember that 1,200 tons of hay/alfalfa takes a lot of men to do two hay crops and at least four crops of alfalfa."

"I know and you can hire more men if necessary. Plus, let's not forget that 1,200 tons is worth $24,000, and we accept that it takes money to make money. So, hire all the seasonal workers you need."

Hannah had been sitting by and absorbing everything. She knew that this business was growing, and by being the office manager, she would be able to keep up. Hannah had an idea. "To simplify the two ranches' accounting, can we name each ranch and avoid calling the new one the Klaus ranch. How about Ranch-1 and Ranch-2?"

With a double approval, Jake then changed the subject to discussing individual employees. "How are the Belcher boys working out.?"

"Couldn't be happier with them. They are good cultivators, and handle all harvesting equipment as experts. They'll do any job, but are the best on the mowers and plows, which are the more difficult jobs."

"They are reliable, trustworthy, good with horses, and can eat like two men. I would like to change their employment from seasonal to year-round."

"Agree, now how about the three would be rapists." As Hannah tensed up, Clayton added, "you mean, Daryl, Merle and Enis?"

"Yes, and we didn't know their names!"

"Well, right now they are busy hauling that 100-year old manure pile at Ranch-2. That is a well fermented pile and the weeds will be inactive. They are now spreading it on the newly cultivated acres. These men have become valuable. They are great with horses and agricultural implements. When we need extra cowhands, they are always the first to volunteer and they get along with everybody. I'm afraid to ask, but we could make them year-round workers if you agree."

Hannah added, "with their past history, do you have any worries about their character?"

"Anytime I'm asked that question, I refer to my four reliable observers, Rocky, the two foremen, and the cook. In this case, they have all supported these three guys without reservations."

Hannah was happy to say, "that's good enough for me. What do you think Jake?" "I agree."

"Now, what about Dempsey Peabody?"

"He's one of my most effective cowhands. He has plenty of experience with the roundup, calving season and is great herding cattle. I'm expecting a lot from him this season. He also was an eager worker during the harvesting season. He's going to make a great addition to our staff. Besides, he likes cooking and is a great help to our cook."

"Finally, how is dad settling in?"

"He has found his retirement calling in working the crops. He works all day every day. He has become adept with plowing to seeding. When there is no work, he volunteers to drive the manure spreader to the fields as the three boys load up the second manure spreader. I try to give him two days off every week, but sometimes I'm overruled. The man is happy, and you don't have to worry about him."

"That's it for me, got anything else?"

"Yes, one more. We need our own part-time resident blacksmith. We have many horses that need to be reshod, wagons that need wheels repaired, and implements that need steel work and welding. It involves too many man hours and equipment downtime to keep bringing our jobs to the two blacksmiths in town. Besides, they are too busy to spend two days a week to come to our ranches."

"I certainly agree with you if we have two days of work per week.

But where do we find a smithy?"

"It so happens, when the town blacksmiths are overloaded with work, they send the extra work to Stanley Washington. He's a homesteader three miles east of us that has a side business since his kids take care of the cattle and crops. When I spoke to him about taking on the job, he wasn't at all interested. When I told him it was your ranch, he immediately changed his mind and said he would come two days a week starting as soon as we get him the tools of the trade. Is there any reason why he changed his mind when he heard your name."

"Oh, I recall where the name comes from. His wife works for the Newmanns on our egg enterprise. I remember now, I served a foreclosure on him but instead of evicting him, I gave him $2,000 from the Benefactor Fund to get his mortgage and creditors paid off, and vary and increase his crops. I guess he's done well and even started a side business of blacksmithing to supplement his income."

"Wow, that explains everything and the fact that he doesn't want any pay till he repays his debt to you."

"The man has no debt to repay as the money given to him came from my Benefactor Fund. Don't let him have his way, check with the town blacksmiths to find what would be an average wage and pay him an extra 25% to come to us to do the work. Now let's look at what he needs for tools and supplies."

"Mr. Washington suggests a small addition to the barn as the blacksmith shop with its own coal bin. The main items are the forge with a bellows, extra-large elevated vice, a London Anvil with a flat and curved horn and 'Hardy' holes. The other tools of the trade include: Assorted tongs, assorted 'Hardy' tools including a 'Hardy' chisel, set of hand hammers, peen hammer, anvil devil for horseshoes, bending forks, quenching bucket, large file, hacksaw with blades, assorted rivets, hand chisels-gouges-punches and a blacksmith apron. Last but not least, assorted sizes and lengths of general bar stock to include horseshoe bar stock as well as a complete farrier kit."

Jake was pleasantly surprised as he said, "one thing is for sure, you don't come to these meetings unprepared. That's a complete list. Order everything thru Heinz's hardware and have Cass Construction build a shop addition to the barn." Closing the meeting over coffee, the small talk covered how well the herd looked and the upcoming calving season.

***

The next day, the Duo was called to the drilling site. Emerson started, "good news, feel these stone chips and look and feel the water wash." "Wow, the chips are oily, and the water wash looks brown and feels oily."

"Yes, and if I'm not mistaken, we should feel a rumble soon."

A half hour later, the earth started to shake, and a roar followed that kept increasing in intensity as a black geyser appeared pushing the drill out of the well. Oil was gushing out and hit the deflector shield throwing the crude north of the derrick. The Duo was hugging and jumping with joy as they got covered with the black gold.

In a short time, the gusher was capped and a pressure gauge on the cap revealed a pressure consistent with 100 barrels per day. Hannah exclaimed, "we started with 2500 acres, we're changing our herd to crossbreeds, developed a crop business, established a Marshal Service, and then increased our acreage to just under 14,000 acres. Clayton said we had a mega ranch; I say with an oil well, we now have an EMPIRE. Where do we go from here?"

"We'll dig a second well and then let things plateau for a while."

"Really, what have you got in mind."

"The Peabodys are here and we'll try to hire them to dig another well before they leave."

***

For the next week, things happened quickly. Emerson set up the receiving station and transfer pump, as Hayden got the transfer pipes connected. With the system connected they started filling oak barrels and loading them onto boxcars. With the production at 100 barrels per day, the men were filling a boxcar with 100 barrels each day. In three days, the duo signed three contracts with private refineries and the first three boxcars were in route at 70 cents per barrel.

During this time Jake was in contact with

a barrel manufacturer in Missouri to supply them with 1,500 barrels. Fortunately, half of that order arrived in three days—just in time to continue receiving the oil. In the meantime, Hayden convinced Jake to construct a holding shed at the railroad yard to store empty and filled barrels until orders came in. Cass was working overtime, with every employee, to construct a wood floor shed in a matter of days. When completed, it measured 50X100 feet and would hold 1,000 barrels.

As Emerson was tearing down the derrick, a final boxcar arrived with funny looking parts. Hayden said that Dutton's last item on his order was to deliver a pump-jack or a "nodding donkey" as it was commonly known. This included a heavy steel head, a walking beam and a steam powered plant in the rear. The entire structure looked like a horse or donkey and was stored in a rainproof shed next to the well. It was kept in reserve if the well's production went below 50 barrels per day.

The last issue was hiring workers. A total of six men were hired, two at the well and four at the receiving station. A manually operated hydraulic lift was delivered that allowed two men to move the 42-gallon barrels weighing 300 pounds each. Hayden trained the men to do their jobs independently.

With everything completed, the Duo went to see the Peabodys. "What happens now?" "Well, we've put some adds in several city newspapers and if we don't get any drilling jobs, we'll pack up everything and head back to Denver."

"Could it be that your ads haven't had enough time to get the word out?"

"We'll give it another week while we load the derrick, drill, bulldozer, tent city and miscellaneous tools."

"Let us offer you an alternative. The best advertisement you can have is two successful oil wells on your record. Hannah will prepare an article, for the local paper, on the goings on during the drilling of this well, and send it to Dallas, Houston, Amarillo, Lubbock, Brownsville and El Paso. While the article circulates, dig us a second well"

The Peabodys were both pensive and

Emerson finally spoke. “Well, that’s not a bad idea since all our equipment is here. We could use the same water well by adding a pump and pipeline to the next well site. If we stay within a half mile, a second pump would transfer the oil to the existing line. The receiving station is already rated for processing up to 250 barrels per day. So, it’s doable. It is up to you.”

Hannah had been thinking and said, “is it possible that we would pay for a second well but still end up with only a total of 100 barrels per day since each well would drop its production by 50%.”

“No!” “Why?” “Because an untapped reservoir will hold its production until a crucial amount of oil has been removed. Then, with the reservoir pressure down, each and all wells will simultaneously drop their yield to require a ‘donkey’ well pump to maintain a high yield. Two wells don’t change the ‘total’ oil yield before a pump is needed.”

Everyone was silent and obviously thinking. Hayden pulled Emerson aside and they were heard whispering. As they returned, Emerson spoke, "we have a proposition for you. If the next well comes within 800 feet, we'll give you a 20% discount off the standard rate since our equipment is already on site. Any drilling beyond 800 feet is free up to 1000 feet. If we drill beyond 1,000 feet, the rate increases to $55 per foot. If the well never comes in at our 1,500-foot maximum range, we'll charge you only $5,000. That's how certain we are that the well will come in."

Hannah did some quick calculations and said "500 feet at $25 per foot is $12,500 and let's say another 300 feet at $40 per foot is another $12,000. $24,500 minus 20% comes to +- $20,000." Jake looked at Hannah who gave him the nod. "It's a deal, come to my office and we'll sign a contract. I'll give you a deposit of $5,000 since it covers the minimum charge if the well never comes in."

***

The days went by and the Peabodys had chosen a flat area, with a lot of oil seepage, and only a quarter mile from the first well. The derrick was almost completed, and drilling was scheduled to start tomorrow.

Meanwhile, at the Circle G Ranch, Galvin was meeting with the five regulators he had hired from the Houston area. "I'm surprised you agreed to take this job since it doesn't pay much in advanced fees. Do you have an ulterior motive?" "Yes, the first is because we'll be robbing the bank after the monthly payroll arrives. The second is because this Harrison pushed us out of Austin last winter when he arrested several of our friends, of which several hanged, and the others went to prison." "Well that's good. Here is your advance payment of $1,000 and make sure no one knows that I set you up for this robbery. Remember Captain, before you leave the bank make sure that everyone hears this line. . . . . Harrison!"

Two days later, the Duo got up late because of extensive intimate activity. After a replenishing breakfast of corned beef hash, with poached eggs, toasted fresh bread and coffee, a rider was heard entering the yard at a full gallop. Tommy jumped off and flew over the porch while pushing the front door in. "Marshal, there's been a robbery at the Ranchers Bank, Sheriff Bixby and his deputy have been wounded and a teller has been killed. The sheriff is requesting your help"

"Hannah ring the bell six times and then go saddle your horse while you wait for Willie and Furman." Jake grabbed his sawed-off shotgun and his long-range Win 76 and rushed to the barn to get his horse. Rocky and Red Flower had responded to the six-bell alarm and already had Jake's and Rocky's horses saddled. Coming out of the barn at a full gallop; Red Flower stood in awe with a heart full of pride.

The street in front of the bank was full of people gathering. Jake went inside and Doc Craven was finishing with the dead clerk. Thurman Greathouse was beside himself. "Thurman, get a hold and tell me what happened. Four men came in demanding all the cash. Once the drawers were emptied, the leader wanted the vault opened. When I refused, he turned around and shot George in the face—in cold blood. It's all my fault and I ended up opening the vault anyways. Now George is dead."

"Things like this happen all the time. Even if you had opened the vault right away, the outlaw would likely have shot someone else before leaving. Now, what did they take?" "$5,000 of our funds and the $10,000 payroll. We're ruined and George is gone. Why? How did they know the payroll was arriving today."

"A spy in your bank, the railroad or anyone else in town. Especially a rancher who knew his funds would be available today to pay his men. But that's for later. Anything else to add?" "Yes, as the gang leader left, he yelled out—'you can blame this robbery on Jake Harrison!'"

"Well that helps, now I know who to suspect. Where do I find the sheriff?" "He's at the City Hospital with his deputy, they both will be needing surgery." As he left, he saw Rocky checking out the outlaw tracks.

Rushing into the emergency section of the

City Hospital, Doc Craven had just pulled out the bullet from Herbs shoulder and was closing he wound after probing and flushing the area with carbolic acid. "Doc how is the deputy? "He was shot in the knee and will need surgery, but he'll be alright. That lady in the other room may never recover." "Who is she?" "Myra Gunther, George's widow with three kids, and she's my office nurse."

"I'll see to her needs, later Doc."

"Herb, is there anything you can tell me about this gang?"

"Yes, the gang leader rides a white stallion with four black boots and a black mane/tail. You can't miss it and the man's name is Captain Tucker from Houston. He and his gang are wanted for murder and bank robberies all over Texas. I recalled the wanted posters because of that marked horse. When the gang left, they took the east trail out of town likely heading for Austin. We both got shot when we tried to stop them as they rode by the office. We didn't get any, but they got us."

As they were still talking, Hannah and the

squad were arriving. Hannah said, "Rocky found something worth tracking." Rocky explained in his usual short English, "one horse is favoring the left rear leg. Horse get lame in short time. The hoofprint from that leg are not as deep and I can follow it."

Tracking five horses with a marked hoofprint was easy while the outlaws were traveling in the main road. When they stepped off the trail and traveled cross country, the pace slowed down. They followed for the next three hours when Rocky said, "this is good sign, the horse with a bad leg is now lame. Rider has doubled up with another rider and their tracks are much deeper with two men riding. The lame horse will force them to stop, take shelter or set up camp. We 'get' them now, boss!"

About an hour later, several shots were heard and then nothing. Jake said, "sounds like that gang got some temporary resistance. I hope we don't find any bodies other than some gang members." The squad stopped, tethered their horses, took their rifles and their sawed-off shotguns and walked along the tracks. At 300 yards an old dilapidated shack and a lean-to appeared in a small clearing. The squad hid behind the tree line and watched the cabin with their 50X binoculars. Jake added, "well boys, we'll wait till dark or sooner if they drink themselves in a stupor, then we'll rush the cabin."

Rocky was clearly upset, "look, the horses were left at the railing without water and still saddled. Lame horse is standing on three legs and they do nothing for leg. I hate men that abuse their mounts." When Rocky turned around to the squad, he saw Jake looking up in the trees. "Boss, why you looking in trees?"

Furman then informed Rocky, Willic and Walt. "You see, when Jake was a junior Deputy Marshal, we were about to rush a cabin full of outlaws. Just before the attack, Jake shows up with a huge hornet's nest in a burlap bag. At darkness, he opened the outlaw's door, took the nest out of the bag, rapped it against the door frame, threw it in the camp and closed the door. Now, let your imagination go wild, and you won't even be close to what happened. Every time I think about that day, I start laughing again. So, I guess he's looking for another hornet's nest, heh?" Rocky was thinking and finally said, "that good idea, I go for walk and come back with nest before it get dark."

Hours go by and the squad is having a cold snack of crackers, cheese and jerky. They were not paying attention and Rocky snuck up without being seen. Suddenly, Rocky speaks, "bang, bang, bang, bang, you all dead except boss lady." When the squad turned to look at Rocky they all exclaimed, "Jeezes, get rid of that thing, that's not a nest, what in hell is wrong with you, you're going to get us all sprayed—THAT'S A DAMN SKUNK."

"Yes, matter of fact it angry male, will make great hornet's nest. It 'not spray' because I hold animal by tail and they not spray if cannot lift tail—old Indian trick. We wrap it against door frame, make more angry and bite like a cat, throw it in camp, lock door and run like hell. We all have good time, and we no get hurt, heh. I like that white man word—heh?"

Hannah started laughing and then everyone

followed suit. Hannah added between her chortles, "I thought being a marshal was dangerous work, hell, this is the most fun I've had in months.

I can't wait till nightfall comes. Jake finally adds, "Rocky, if this works and we don't get shot at, you'll get a bonus."

"No, this job bring back my pride and honor. Happy to help. Give bonus to wife of dead bank clerk. That sad!"

***

At darkness, the squad made their way to the cabin. They came upon the body of an old man who had been shot. As they approached the cabin, loud snoring was easily heard. The boys walked the horses away from the cabin as Rocky and Jake stepped to the front door. When it was realized that the door opened onto the porch, Jake quickly made shim to fit under the door. Rocky wrapped the skunk on the door frame as it hissed with teeth showing. In a joint motion, Rocky throws the skunk in the cabin as Jake shims the door so it cannot open. Quickly they moved back in the trees with the rest of the squad to await the results of one unhappy full-size male skunk.

***

Minutes passed and nothing was happening. Each squad member was glancing at each other wondering what happened with that animal. Rocky finally whispered, “cat needs eyes adjusted to see outlaws in full darkness. Wait, fun about to start.”

Suddenly, the cabin came alive. “Ouch, something bit me, it’s just a rat, Aaaahh, something bit my big toe, who let a cat in here, jeese there is an animal in here, will someone light a lamp and shoot that thing, with the lamp on--oh no it’s got a white streak. What, that’s a skunk as the animal lifted its tail and sprayed a full dose of scent all over the camp. Outlaws were screaming, I can’t see, my eyes are shut, I’m choking, let’s get out of here, we can’t the door is locked, shoot the lock off, there isn’t any, shoot the hinges off, get out thru the windows, there aren't any. Even with the bottom hinge blown off, the door's shim held.

Finally, a foot punched out a wall board, followed by a second and third. Men were crawling over each other and fighting to get out. After several got their union suits torn off on nails sticking out, the five men ended up on the ground rubbing their eyes and spreading the skunk's juices even more. As Jake was about to warn them not to rub their eyes, the angry skunk came flying out of the camp and landed in the middle of the five outlaws. Still getting revenge, the skunk continued to bite every body-part imaginable including their private areas.

Hannah was laughing so loud that she was sitting on the ground. "I would never have believed this if I had not seen it myself." Furman added, "you haven't seen anything yet, keep watching." No one had seen another skunk arrive, presumably its mate, and decided to help her mate. She turned her behind and sprayed the bunch as her mate joined her and left the area. The men were screaming even louder. One outlaw said, "will someone get a gun and shoot me. I've lost the tip of my tally-wacker, and I'll never see again. Another yelled, no more-no more, I give up." Then all five outlaws could see the lawmen standing over them, including a woman laughing out of control.

Jake finally spoke. "You are all under arrest for robbery and murder. Stand up and strip out of those union suits. You're going in the river with lye soap and you're not coming out till you no longer stink." As the men threw their union suits in the camp, they walked in the buff some 100 yards to the river.

While following the group to the river, Hannah was heard whispering to Jake, "I didn't realize that thumb size was the manhood standard. Guess you're a bit over endowed, hey?"

"Well, you have to realize that what these men just experienced was not exactly foreplay. In face of stress, organ selection comes first and when they were bitten and sprayed, sex response was not utmost on their mind. That's why they are all sporting a dangling mini, heh?"

"Yes, and I have to find the words to add this scene and appearances in my book. I think I'll use the skunk instead of the hornet's nest, but then there might be a second book!"

While the outlaws were scrubbing, the squad went thru the saddlebags on their horses. Three clean union suits and two pairs of pants were found. After they passed the "fresh" smell test, they were allowed to partially dress and then manacles were applied to their wrists and ankles. Each outlaw was secured to their own tree as a fire was started to cook the squad's supper.

The saddlebags revealed the undivided bank heist of $15,000. Other saddlebags also revealed a total of +-$4,000. Jake separated $1,000 as Rocky's bonus, and would be given to Myra Gunther as previously agreed. Each squad member got $500. Plus, time would tell if the bank would post a reward and whether there were any wanted posters on this bunch.

While Hannah was preparing supper of canned beef stew and canned beans with coffee, Walt asked what they were going to do about the five pistols left in the camp. Jake answered, "it's going to be years before anyone can use this structure, so, we'll burn it along with its contents after we bury this old gentleman."

Willie's ears perked up and said, "I know several cowhands and crop workers that don't have any firearms. I'll go in, pick up the pistols, soak them in water/lye soap and clean them up. They won't smell anything when I'm done with them, but the leather holsters will stay in the camp."

Jake added, "in that case, take their five rifles/scabbards off their horses, and hand them out to the cowhands. If anyone is left without a firearm, send them to Blackwell's Gun Shop and have them pick up, on my account, at least one firearm—pistol, rifle or shotgun."

With time to spare before supper, the other squad members offered to help Willie with the cleaning job. They had three buckets ready as a progressive cleaning solution and in no time, the five pistols were left to dry and would be oiled after supper. Jake commented to Hannah, "look at those men, they are all $500 richer, yet they spend a stinking time to save a total of

$125 for their cowhand and crop friends. That's well-placed values, if I say so myself!"

Supper turned out to be the best event of the day. Everyone enjoyed the stew and beans as well as the canned peaches for dessert. When supper was done, one of the outlaws demanded water and some food. Jake stepped up to the leader and said, "you must be the one known as Captain Tucker?"

"Yes, so what?" "Well, let me tell you how things are going to be. Until you get to jail, you have no benefits or rights. Look at it as you're a hog-tied captured predator animal. You don't get water or food and you don't get unmanacled so you can relieve yourselves. And we're not helping you with your call to nature. Do it in your pants."

"We'll help you to get on your horse, but the ankle manacle will be locked onto one stirrup. If you fall off your horse, or chose to commit suicide by jumping off, then you will die a horrible death as your horse drags you and steps on you."

"But that's not humane treatment like you lawmen are supposed to follow."

"You are not human. You are an evil spirit that has run a reign of terror over good people. You killed George Gunther just to get money. Now, who is going to support his wife—as if you care. And that's the last I will say to you. You all listen, the next man who utters a single word will get a visit from that Apache Indian and you'll lose your tongue, and that is a promise."

Things were quiet for the remainder of the evening, and except for the Duo, the squad got a full night's sleep. The Duo was sleeping in a double bedroll situated 50 yards from camp. Hannah's hand was teasing and tantalizing Jake. When the wang wallet exploded, Hannah was finally satisfied.

The next morning, Jake had an idea. "Tucker, who put you up to this bank robbery?" "Go to hell, no food, no water, no talking."

Without a single word, Jake took out his awl and sat on the next outlaw and shoved the point in the unsuspecting outlaw's bad molar. The result was spectacular. The outlaw had a full bladder and while he was screaming like he was stuck in a bear trap, he thoroughly wet himself. After he was done with the first outlaw, he moved along to the other three and gave them the same treatment with the same results.

When Jake got to the last one, Captain Tucker quickly volunteered the fact that Grant Galvin had paid them $1,000 and had told them of the payroll's arrival. Jake last words to the entire bunch was, "you're going to get your trial, and if you don't want to hang, you might consider turning state's evidence by signing a statement against Galvin. It's your neck or your life, and going against the hanging Judge Hobart is a foregone conclusion if you don't have some type of amnesty."

At the end of the day, the caravan arrived and each of the outlaws smelled of urine. Sheriff Bixby arranged some clean clothes and put the outlaws in their cage. Jake handed President Greathouse the $15,000 and then had a private talk with him.

"Did you ever post a reward for the monies' return?"

"Yes, $1,000 and I will give you the cash today."

"What happens to Mrs. Gunther and her three kids?"

"She gets George's death benefit of $2,000 since George died on the job. She still owes the bank $719 on their mortgage but I will pay that off trying to stem my grief. Otherwise, she'll need to continue working for Doc Craven unless she remarries to someone with money.

However, not too many men want a ready-made family."

"I see, so add the reward money to the death benefit, give me a bank voucher for an extra $2,000 out of my Benefactor Fund, and give me the total bank draft of $5,000 in Myra's name. I'll deliver the draft today."

"Certainly, and that's very generous of you Jake."

"No, it's just partial justice for that lady and the kids."

***

Later that day, the Duo knocked at the Gunther home. "Welcome Marshals, please come in. I hear that you caught my husband's killers."

Hannah answered, "Yes, and justice will be handed out by Judge Hobart. Jake and I commiserate with you for your loss. Now, what happens with you and your kids?"

"My kids are 8,10 and 14 years old. The oldest, Sophie does well leading the two young ones and they can care for themselves after school. I work for Doc Craven from school time to 5PM daily. I need to work for my sanity and for supporting myself. Doc Craven is very generous and pays me $50 per month. With a mortgage payment it's going to be tight money wise, but we'll manage till Sophie is old enough to earn some part-time work in Natalie's Diner."

Jake adds, "that sounds good. Realizing we cannot undo your husband's loss, please accept this cumulative bank drafts to help you achieve some financial security."

Myra looks at the drafts and starts crying. "Oh goodness, where does this money come from, I don't know anyone on earth who has $6,000 to give away."

"Well you have the right to know. $2,000 is your husband's insurance death benefit with the bank. $1,000 comes from our Marshal squad forfeiting the bank's reward for returning the stolen money. $2,000 comes from the Harrison Benefactor Fund for victims of violent crimes and $1,000 comes from a crazy Apache Indian who forfeited his bonus to help you. Now that covers the $6,000 but President Greathouse is paying off your mortgage of $719 out of his pocket. There are many people who want to guarantee that you and your kids will survive."

Myra eventually stopped crying and had a nice visit with the Duo. When her kids arrived from school, the Duo took their exit. On the way home, Hannah asks, "what happens now?" "We need to do something about Galvin, his first attempt at revenge will not be the last. I want to get Judge Hobart's thought on the matter before we decide what to do."

***

CHAPTER 7

A FULL PLATE

The next day, while Hannah was attending her weekly writing class, Jake went around the town businesses that held a credit account for the ranch. Jake was settling the accounts as well as depositing cash in advance. Sheriff Bixby found Jake walking about town. "Glad I found you. The five outlaws had wanted posters on them, and I collected $3,250 on Western Union vouchers." Jake took the vouchers and handed Herb $250. "This is for paying the jailer, continue to maintain your deputy's salary, and what other expenses you have on the matter."

Before he picked up Hannah, Jake deposited

the reward money in all five accounts and brought four receipts to give to his men. When Hannah came out of class, they were planning to get an early supper at Natalie's when the Duo recognized Dutton and Isabella Peabody standing at the railroad yard. The Duo stepped over and said, "Commandant, what brings you to town, you folks are a long-ways from Denver?"

Isabella spoke first, "we wanted to see our son and thought to surprise him with our unscheduled appearance."

"Well, your sudden appearance will certainly surprise not just your son but will also surprise Emerson and Hayden."

"What are those two doing here. They wired me that they had hit a gusher and would head back to Denver a week ago."

"Well, you see, I made them an offer they couldn't refuse. They are drilling us a second well to add to their record before abandoning Texas as an oil state. Hannah has ads all over the big Texas city newspapers in areas known to have oil strikes. They are hoping to get in the Texas oil boom in its early stages."

Hannah added, "so why don't you join us at the ranch for supper. I'll put a pork roast in the oven, you can visit with your family this afternoon, and then join us for supper. That will be the beginning of our thanks for sending your brothers to dig our well. We are indebted to you and will try to find a way to repay you."

Isabella jumped in, "nonsense, it is us who will forever be indebted to you. But we would love to spend some time and have supper with you."

"Great, throw your luggage in our buggy, we'll drop them off at your hotel, and then we'll bring you to our ranch—the Circle H Ranch."

Upon their arrival, Clayton informed the Peabodys that Dempsey was fencing on the far northeast corner, and being on the late team, would not be back till dark. Then he added, "however, I just saw your two brothers heading for their office in tent city and it's just a short walk from here. I bet they'll be surprised to see you folks."

After a long visit with the Peabody brothers, Dutton and Isabella joined the Duo for a visit. Hannah gave them a tour of the house and almost didn't include her writing room suspecting this would not be of any interest to them. When Isabella saw a typewriter thru the doorway, Hannah could not believe the Peabody's interest.

Dutton started, "what on earth are you up to with piles of typed pages, and with a carbon copy. Hannah answered, "I've decided to try my hand at writing a novel of these times out west." Isabella was walking around Hannah's library and said, "I see you have a current and updated Encyclopedia Britannica, an unabridged Webster's dictionary, a Roget's Thesaurus, an Old West History textbook as well as the most popular classics, novels and western dime novels. Who reads these books, especially the classics, and who uses these reference manuals?"

Jake spoke, "Hannah has read every book on the shelf, and does her research thru these reference books. She has been attending the college taking courses in composition, typing and now writing techniques for her novel. She is on page 187 of a proposed 300-page novel. She has finished Book 1&2, and is about to start Book 3 to tie in the first two books."

Dutton and Isabella looked at each other and Dutton said, "Do you know what we do for a living"

Jake said, "Well you're the Lawman School's Commandant, and we figured you're independently wealthy when we found out you had brought $50,000 to ransom Dempsey and did not take a salary to work at the Lawman School."

"That is all correct, but we inherited Isabella's parents' business. We are book publishers. We either charge a fee to publish and market your book or we buy the book outright from a writer and publish/market it as a speculation."

Hannah had her hand on her mouth, "Goodness, you're the famous and prestigious publishing firm called 'Osmer and Peabody' of Denver!"

Isabella added, "well, I am a descendant of the Osmer family dating back to England.

Would you allow me to bring Book 1&2 to our hotel. I would so much enjoy reading your work. Right now, I am reviewing a rather boring story and would appreciate a break from the only manuscript I brought along on this trip."

"Oh, please do. Remember that this is my first work and I would appreciate and accept any criticism as constructive. For now, I only have my writing instructor to guide me, and he sometimes allows too much leeway so as not to discourage one from writing. I look forward to hearing your assessment."

Supper was a success. It had started with Hannah's homemade onion soup. The main course was roast pork with mashed potatoes, turnip, pork gravy and buttered rolls. Dessert was bread pudding over tea or coffee. Dutton was especially pleased with the roast while Isabella was a bit surprised how delicious the onion soup was. At the end of the meal, while visiting in the parlor, Dempsey was heard knocking at the front door. Hannah got up to answer the door and said, "hello Dempsey, we have some guests who would like to see you."

Dempsey was almost in tears to see his parents. The Duo excused themselves to the kitchen to start the cleanup, thereby allowing some private time for the Peabodys. It was left that Dempsey would drive his parents back to their hotel and continue sharing their time together. The Peabodys decided to stay four more full days in town when their son changed his work schedule to days. That freed him at 3PM and would spend his evenings showing his parents the town and the ranch.

The third day, Dutton and Isabella arrived after breakfast. Isabella handed Hannah her working manuscript and said, "my dear, this is a fantastic story, it is well written, and I can't wait to see what happens in Book 3. Dutton added, "the story is what people down east want to read about realistic activities in the west. There is no exaggeration, yet there is some fantastic sex, humor, shoot-em-up and justice."

Isabella added, "of course, you know what men like. What I liked the most is how you developed the two main characters' personalities. I simply identified with the heroine, and that takes a natural talent to accomplish this with the written word."

The Duo was listening to every word. Hannah was on the verge of tears and Jake realized how proud he was of his lovely talented wife. It was Dutton who finally summarized things, "we have enjoyed these two books and know you are writing a winner and a keeper. So, we have a special proposition for you. We would like to publish and market your book. We will use our Denver office for marketing it out west, and we'll send the published version to our other office in Boston. You wrote this masterpiece; we'll do all the work to print and market it. And we split the profit 50-50, forever. We are so certain that this story will sell that we are ready to give you an advance of $5,000 on your share of the profits. Either way, we are all going to make money."

"OMG, I have been vindicated. Now I know that I can do this and will continue with the same format and writing style. The deposit is not necessary, and I'm willing to take my chances with the profits. As a thank-you for believing in me, if this first book is profitable, you will get to publish my future books."

Dutton said, "then let's sign this standard contract with the variations mentioned, and we will take your two-book manuscript with us. Since you already edited it, the printer will set your words to type and start printing it. By the time you send us the next book, the printer will be ready for it. If for any reason you get delayed or sidelined, the printer will work on whatever you send him."

"Thank you. Out of curiosity, which caper did you enjoy the most." "Isabella liked the skunk in the cabin siege. I liked the one where the gang drank whiskey laced with syrup of ipecac and a horse laxative. Wow. I wasn't there, but the writer surely made me think I was there to smell the results. It's not always the content that makes a good read, but the words used to describe the content—and that's what makes a top writer."

Isabella asked, "can you give us a hint on what the final book will look like?"

"Well, it's pretty obvious that the hero and

heroine will meet, and you can expect humor, love, intimacy and so much more. Plus, I am working on two classic bounty hunting capers that involve kidnaping and jungle warfare. I think you'll enjoy Book 3."

***

A few days later, the drilling had reached 300 feet. Jake had a planning meeting with the Peabody brothers. "Assuming this well comes thru, I'm going to need a manager to deal with the private refineries, railroad shipments, returning empty barrels, and maintaining a full employment roster of laborers. There is plenty of available laborers in town, but where do I get an educated oil man with a business sense to be the manager in charge?"

Hayden hesitated and even looked at Emerson. "You might as well mention Greg's name." Hayden agreed, "we have such a man who is ready for such a position and responsibility. The problem is that we have that same position filled with a very capable man of twenty years.

We hate to admit it, but Greg Webb will not wait any longer."

"Is this a man who could live in a small town, or does he need the life around a big city?"

"We don't know, all we know is that he gets cleaned up and goes into town every night. Some of the guys think he's met someone special, but he won't admit to anything. We think you need to have a sit down with him and see what's what. As much as we don't want to lose him, if it's going to happen, then let it be here and not a drilling competitor."

Days later Hannah had a longer than usual writing lesson. Jake had also been asked to see Judge Hobart the same day. Jake dropped Hannah off and rode the buggy to the courthouse. "Come in Jake, we have a rather unusual problem in a silver mining community some 30 miles north of San Antonio. According to city Marshal Brisco, there is a mole that keeps sending letters to him regarding the dangerous working conditions in the mine as well as murders of small claim owners east of the 'TDSM'—short for Texas Dutch Silver Mine."

"The acclaimed owner is Dutch by the name of Del VanHouten. He employs 150 workers who work in two shifts. There is a small town that supports the basic needs of its workers but at a high price for local convenience. There is a 'TDSM' bank, mercantile, butcher shop, hardware, saloon and livery. The only major business that is not owned by VanHouten is the post office, telegraph, railroad and the local doc."

"What about a lawman in town?"

"Unfortunately, there is no one. VanHouten has a bunch of regulators that wear a badge imprinted with 'VanHouten Security.' These men have not investigated the killings of small claim owners and the mole is claiming that they are the ones killing the small miners."

"So, what we have is the claim that someone is killing miners who have small claims, and the mine is operating under dangerous conditions. The mine's owner is not seeing to mine safety and the security agents are suspected of being the murderers. Presumably, for the benefit of Mister Del VanHouten, heh?"

"It appears that, in a nutshell, your assumptions are probably correct."

"This requires detective work more than the full firepower of my complete squad. I will go with Willie and Furman and see if we can get a better idea of the goings on and try to identify this mole. We need the mole's help, or we'll be butting heads against the mine's stone walls."

"We'll need help regarding dangerous mining operations. We don't know the acceptable safe norm. So, can you arrange for a Federal mining inspector to assist us. We will enforce whatever this inspector demands. It could be as simple as fines or structural changes, but if we have a life-threatening situation, we'll close the mine down."

"I'll arrange for one to meet you when your train arrives!"

"Before I leave, we need to decide what to do with Grant Galvin. You know about the two outlaws who have signed a statement implicating Galvin in paying them to rob our bank."

"Yes, and I'm prepared to send them to Huntsville for turning state's evidence. However, bringing Galvin to trial will likely be a failure. Galvin will have an attorney who will argue that this is outlaws blaming Galvin to get a reduced sentence. It will also be 'he said-he said' type of argumentative evidence. With his status among ranchers, we'll never get a conviction and we won't be able to bring up the charges again. That would fall in the 'double jeopardy' category. You need to convince him that he has to cease this revenge avenue, or he will again end up in prison. This time, it will be much more than 30 days."

"Changing his mind may be difficult, but we'll try."

***

That evening the Duo had their private time when they got to talk about upcoming events. Jake told Hannah about the trip to San Antonio. Hannah interrupted him and said, "recently, I noticed some strange bumps surrounding my nipples. When I showed them to your mother, she smiled and just said I needed to see Doc Craven. So, I went to my writing class and afterwards I had a visit with Doc Craven. It seems that I'm not ill. I am pregnant and about 10 weeks along."

Jake eyebrows pulled up and then his lips turned up in a smile. "Hannah, you're with child?" "Yes." "With our baby?" "Well of course it's ours!" Jake jumped up and hugged his wife. "Are you happy?" "Oh, very much so. But the doctor wants me to take it easy for a month since this is a sensitive time to establish a good pregnancy. So, I think I should skip this assignment just to be safe."

"Are you suspecting something is not quite right?" "No, I'm fine and Doc Craven said so. And don't get it in your head that we have to stop having relations either. Doc Craven said it was Ok."

"Well, maybe I can tone down my aggressiveness."

"That's ok, as long as the endpoint is the same."

"Now let's talk turkey, when you joined

the squad, we had agreed that if you ever got pregnant, that you would quit the squad. Do you still agree?"

"Yes, under one condition." "Which is?" "That you review every assignment in detail so I can use the caper in my book."

"Will do. Now for your duties. You need more help with household duties."

"Oh, that's not going to be a problem. I'm sure that your mom and Laura will be over me and I'll likely not be allowed to take my own bath or get dressed by myself."

"And what about Josie, Sandra or Camilla?"

"I may be wrong, but I suspect that those three are also in the same 'gravid' situation as I am."

"Assuming 'gravid' means pregnant, I wonder if there is something causative with the water or the air?"

"Heck no, it's all about that explosive wang wallet, again!"

"To finish the current events. When a partial squad is gone to San Antonio, you'll probably be here when the second oil well comes in.

Tomorrow, the full squad, minus you, will be visiting Galvin. We are trying to convince him not to continue seeking some revenge against us. Judge Hobart feels we don't have enough to take him to trial with the two outlaws turning state's evidence. He feels that a visit from the full squad of US Marshals will convince him to 'cease and desist.'"

"Why did you say a partial squad was going to San Antonio?"

"I'll explain that when I return from the Circle G Ranch."

***

The next day, five US Marshals turned in the access road to the Circle G ranch-house. All five had their sawed-off shotguns on their backs as a deterrent to interference from the cowhands. Tying the horses' reins on the railing, they were greeted by a man who introduced himself as foreman Kevin Wood. "Good morning Marshals, what brings you to the Circle G Ranch?"

"We have business with Mister Galvin."

"He's in his office with the head gunman he keeps on his coattail. Be careful, that's a bad dude and don't anyone turn your backs on him."

"How many more gunmen does he have?"

"Four, but they're still sleeping from a night of heavy drinking."

"This will not be a friendly social call. Will we have trouble from your cowhands?"

"No sir, we're not involved with the shenanigans going on. That's between the boss and his regulators, as he calls them. The boys and I see nothing, hear nothing and do nothing. Good luck and be careful. The boss is not in a good mood."

Jake knocked at the front door and was received by the regulator with, "what do you want, you have no business here."

"We have no business with you, so step aside or we'll arrest you for interfering with our duties. Now bring us to your boss."

The regulator was overwhelmed by the five men and brought the squad to Galvin's office. "Boss, there are five US Marshals here to see you." Galvin never looked up from his desk and said, “I don’t have any business with them, see them out and close the door.”

Jake assessed the situation as dealing with a pig-headed mule that needed to be brought to attention.

He pulled out his awl and swung it full force at Galvin. The awl went thru his shooting hand and impaled itself in the desktop. Galvin’s eyes bugged out of their sockets as a scream to wake the damned shocked the regulator. As a result, he went for his gun. Walt had been watching him since he thought his face was familiar. When the regulator’s hand touched the pistol grip, Walt smacked his sap with full force at the regulator’s mouth. The man collapsed to the floor with several teeth erupting out of his mouth. Walt said, “boss, spending so much time as jailer, I review many wanted posters, and this dude is wanted, dead or alive.”

“In that case, put the manacles on him and get the barn wrangler to saddle his horse. He’s going to jail and will meet Judge Hobart.”

Meanwhile, Galvin is bleeding all over his papers and staring at the awl, “pull that thing out, now!" "Oh, I now have your attention. This is the way it's going to be. We know you paid to have the bank robbed and this is your only warning." "Go to hell, you bastard."

Jake knew more convincing was needed. He pried the awl in all directions with louder screaming. Then, he pulled it out and asked his men to wait for him outside. Once the men were gone, with the office door closed, he said, "I know you want revenge for killing your son and humiliating you with jail time, but if you even come close to my wife and parents, I will come back and beat you to death. Do you hear me?"

Holding his bleeding hand, he growled, "kiss my ass, I'll kill you and your wife for this."

"You should not have used the word 'wife.' I was afraid you would say something like that. I guess Judge Hobart was wrong." Jake proceeded to give this idiot the thrashing he needed. He punched him in the face till his eyes were puffy, his lips were lacerated, his nose was flat, and teeth were being spit out. He then kicked him in the ribs several times and finally twisted his leg and tore the knee apart. Galvin then passed out as he lay on the floor.

Coming outside, Kevin asked, "should we get Doc Craven?" "No, put him in a wagon and bring him to the hospital. He's passed out and won't give you much trouble. Be careful with his left leg, he's going to need a cast on his left knee."

***

Arriving at the ranch, he set up a meeting with the squad and asked Hannah, Red Flower, Clayton and his parents to attend. After explaining what happened at the Circle G Ranch, Jake asked for a plan to safeguard Hannah while he, Willie and Furman were on assignment in San Antonio. When everyone realized that three Marshals would be gone, everyone seemed to be in a quandary. It was Rocky who spoke first.

"I have 100 good men at my disposal. Your money has helped so many Indian families, and the men have been asking how they can even begin to repay you. I propose to put ten warriors in hiding around your house at all times. Apaches can hide in open desert and never be seen. No one will ever know they are there, but they will be with a bow and a rifle. Plus, Red Flower will spend the night in the ranch house parlor. No one will harm boss wife."

Hannah added, "Rocky, when will you begin to call me Hannah, Red Flower does?" "Soon, boss lady, soon!"

Amos spoke up, "I like the idea, plus Erna and I will spend the day in your house from daybreak till Red Flower arrives."

Walt was last to speak. "How can I help, boss?"

"You can't this time because you have a jail full of outlaws awaiting trial. This is the last time we have to leave you behind. Start posting the bulletin boards and advertise for a full-time jailer to free you up. We can't expect for the sheriff to take this responsibility like he did today."

With no one speaking, Hannah said, "Jake, I'm very comfortable with this plan and I trust Rocky's judgement, do you?" "Yes, and I'll thank your family personally for their help." "No, it is you who saves my family's honor, they thank you."

"Very good, now to make this legal, Hannah will type an order that, as a Federal US Marshal, I am officially employing your family to guard a Deputy Federal Marshal. Give this order to the Indian agent. That way the Indians will be legally allowed to leave the reservation to perform their Federal duties." "Huum, that good idea, boss!"

***

The US Marshal Trio took the morning train to San Antonio. As they stepped on the platform, there was a man standing with a paperboard placard that spelled Harrison. Jake stepped up and introduced himself and his deputies. "I'm Mortimer Butler, Federal mine inspector for the San Antonio area. I'm pleased to meet you and you come highly recommended by Judge Hobart. What do you say we talk over breakfast at Butch's Diner." "Good idea, we'll get our horses and then you can lead the way."

After ordering a hearty meal, Mortimer started, "first, I have seen the notes sent to Marshal Brisco. The composition is fractionated, and I suspect the whistleblower is a general laborer or a working foreman. Without talking to the whistleblower or to a foreman in private, we'll have trouble getting to the root of the problem. Let's hope the whistleblower identifies himself, or the worker's representative can explain the safety issue. I suggest we first meet with the rep, Stanley Caruthers, and go from there. He will be our ticket to the mine where we can establish the safety issue by using a monitor that measures air quality and oxygen levels."

Jake added, "we'll be your Federal officers to guarantee your security. We can force the mine owner, with the threat to close the mine, to follow your recommendations. Our other duty will be to find the murderer of the three nearby claim owners."

"Good, let me get my buggy and we'll head over there. For your information, VanHouten holds 49% of the stock and the Dutch investors from Norway have 51% of the stock and exert a strong hand on VanHouten."

"Well, that explains the mine's name—TDSM instead of the VanHouten Mine, heh!"

Using the side rail to the mine, the team took seats in the single passenger car. At one end of this car was a steel encased room with a huge steel safe for payroll transport. Jake noticed that the passengers were mostly women loaded with groceries. Mortimer explained that the locals cannot afford to buy food at the TDSM mercantile, and every ore train that leaves the mine is filled with housewives to do their shopping in San Antonio, while the ore cars are dropped off at the smelter—also owned by TDSM."

Their first visit was at the rep's office. When they entered, the rep was visibly surprised and said, "how could you respond so quickly, I filed a safety complaint with the board of mining in Austin only yesterday?" "That complaint has not reached my office; we are here because a legitimate whistleblower has claimed direct evidence of a ignored safety problem and the death of three adjoining miners."

"Oh my, let me show you a copy of my complaint and let's talk."

"Your complaint is in accordance with the whistleblower's complaints."

"As I understand it, an air shaft was dug when the mine got to 750 feet in the mountain. Now at 1,000 feet the air is foul, and workers become exhausted only a few hours in their shift. The older workers cannot work in this atmosphere and have had to miss work. It's a mess and the owner refuses to fix the problem. He claims the fix is too expensive and will continue operations with only young men, of which there are plenty willing to work. That ruins families when 50-year old men are out of work."

Jake adds, "What is the fix?"

Mortimer says, "A second air shaft at 1,000 feet or a ventilating furnace in the original air shaft at 750 feet."

Willie asks, "what is a ventilating furnace?"

"It's a matter of converting the original air shaft into two shafts. One is attached to a coal burning furnace that sucks the foul air to feed the furnace, while the hot stove pipe creates a draft that brings in fresh air. It's a simple principle but often difficult to comprehend, but it works."

"If you're ready, wear this visitor tag, and we'll walk the 1,000 feet to get to the work site." The four men arrived and were greeted by the clerk of the works. He was not happy to see an inspector and three US Marshals. "Now, don't cause trouble, because they'll close this mine down and a hundred men will be out of work."

Stanley rebutted, "so, it's better than 100 men dying from bad air. Better get your priorities straight—mister!"

Mortimer wasn't paying attention but was busy measuring the air quality. He even noted that the canary was alive, but lighting a match showed a very low flame that quickly went out. With his monitor readings completed, he motioned for them to exit. It was clear that the presence of three US Marshals had allowed Mortimer to conduct his tests."

Getting back outside, Mortimer insisted

they needed an emergency meeting with Mister VanHouten. The five men appeared without an appointment. When the secretary said that they would have to return tomorrow with an appointment, Jake stepped up and said, "Ma'am, tell Mister VanHouten that if he doesn't see us immediately, that I will arrest him, place him in manacles and hold him in his own jail for the night till our scheduled appointment tomorrow. I'll wait for his answer."

"Yes Marshal. Please have a seat."

In a minute, the lady came out and said, "Mister VanHouten will see you now."

Walking in, Jake immediately had an instant impression. In front of him was a tall man with a protuberant belly, walking back and forth with his crossed hands behind his back. His gait showed an arrogant swagger and his face showed a snobbish air of superiority.

Mortimer took control of the discussion, "Mister VanHouten, your mine has failed the air quality tests. It shows high levels of carbon monoxide, nitrogen dioxide, Radon, particulate matter, and stone dust as well as small amounts of methane. The most serious deficiency is dangerous low levels of oxygen. It is my duty to inform you that until the problem is rectified, the mine's entrance will be closed, and a Federal court order will be posted for employees to examine."

"I object, you cannot do this. My investors refuse to rectify the situation."

"Sir, you need a second air shaft or a ventilating furnace in the original air shaft. This is not negotiable. So, close the mine and put your workers to work digging another air shaft or the alternative."

"You can't make me; I'll have a hundred workers and a half dozen security men run you out of town."

Jake responded, "That may be so, but when we leave, you and your security men will be with us in manacles. "You'll end up with a prison sentence in Huntsville, your investors will be banned to do business in this state and your employees will be the ones to suffer. You will have learned, too late, a fatal mistake with a permanent ending for you."

"Ok, Ok, Ok. It will be done, but Stanley you'll pay for this."

Mortimer answered, "you're wrong, his complaint will take a week to reach my office. You have a whistleblower amidst your employees. He was right about the mine's air quality, maybe he'll be right about your neighbors' murderers, or does that bother you?"

That evening, they had made reservations for three rooms in the San Antonio Star and after a fine meal in the hotel restaurant, with Stanley and Mortimer, a waiter showed up at their table with a note addressed to Marshal Harrison. Jake asked, "Who gave you this note?

"No one in particular, it was found, by the evening hotel clerk, laying on the front counter."

Jake read the note and said, "gentlemen, the whistleblower is in town. He wants to meet tonight about one mile east of town at a beaver pond situated next to the main road."

Meanwhile at the New Braunfels City Hospital, Grant Galvin was still convalescing after needing surgery on his knee and being treated for an infected hand. He now had a full-length cast and was trying to learn how to get around with crutches. He was in a foul mood and had managed to get a telegram to Houston to hire more regulators. Their leader, Colonel Strickner was meeting with Galvin. "I want you and your four men to set fire to the Harrison ranch-house. Bring enough kerosene to do the job. Do this quietly in the middle of the night. Set the fire and get out. No shooting since you'll have a bunkhouse of angry cowhands shooting at you. When the job is done, come back and I'll pay you your fee of $3,000. *Neither man was aware that Myra Gunther was listening behind the door and would report to Sheriff Bixby.*

After picking up their horses, the squad was on their way to the meeting place. When they got there, a man was standing next to the pond with his back to the road. When they stepped down, the man turned around and everyone was surprised. Jake said, "we know you, you're the clerk of the works we met in the mine."

"Yes, I am the whistleblower. I had to greet

you with the request for the mine inspector to not do anything to close the mine. My name is Wilbur Stannish and thank you for ordering a change in the ventilation. My men will start adding a coal furnace with stove pipe to the outside air in the existing air shaft. We were also told by Mister Butler that if this is not adequate to clean the air, that a second air shaft would be added at 1,000 feet."

"You're welcome, now what can you tell us about these murders?"

"There are five remaining claim owners east of the mine. Three owners, claims 2-4, were killed and their partners sold the claims to VanHouten. The crucial claim is number 1 and when this one falls, the claims 5-8 will follow suit."

"Why does VanHouten want these claims, he has a rich mine that is profitably producing silver, gold, copper and lead?"

"To explain this, let me go back historically. When the mine was first used, the quartz vein was followed west, but it quickly petered out. As you walked in yesterday, you probably noticed that you entered the mine and walked north. Eventually you veered to the northeast and when you reached me, you were walking east. You see, the quartz vein, heading east, is getting larger in size and producing valuable ore with silver at $18/ton and gold at $90/ton. But, within six months, the eastern extension will reach its legal end. If VanHouten doesn't own the eastern small claims, the mine will end operations."

"So, claim #1 is at high risk as next to sell out at any means?"

"Yes, my reliable source claims that, tomorrow night, he will be accosted with beatings and torture to sign a quick claim deed. If he doesn't sign, he will be killed and VanHouten will get the claim by paying the heirs."

"How do you know all this, how reliable is your source?"

"My source is VanHouten's secretary, Lila Stannish, my wife!"

"Oh really?"

"Yes, and she will testify that she heard VanHouten order the executions of claim owners

2-4. You see, the TDSM security guards are the murderers you are looking for."

"Thank you for your help. We'll be there to protect claim owner #1 tomorrow night and will leave town with the security guards and VanHouten himself. By the way, what is claim #1's name?"

"Craig Stannish, my brother!"

***

The next night, the Trio explained to Craig what was expected to happen. The Marshals were waiting at the mine entrance when five riders arrived at Craig's tent. After the TDSM guards rousted him out of his tent and started beating him to sign the quick claim deed, the Marshals rushed the tent site and surprised all five guards with their pistols still holstered. "Stop right there, you're under arrest for aggravated battery, coercion, and murder. Put your hands up and if you go for your gun you will die."

"You can't arrest us, we're the law here."

"You're not lawmen, you are cowards and likely wanted outlaws."

One man knew he was wanted dead or alive and decided to go for his gun in the face of three sawed-off shotguns. Furman saw the man pull out his pistol and quickly shot the guard in the chest. The other four knew they had no choice and put up their hands up in surrender.

The next morning, the Trio showed up at VanHouten's office and after doffing their hats to Lila, barged in his office. VanHouten never got a word out when Jake punched him in the nose and pulled the derringer out of his hand. After being manacled, he was forcibly marched with the four live guards to the passenger car for transport to San Antonio. There, Marshal Brisco would hold them till Judge Hobart's arrival for their trial and would gather the reward money on the four guards per their reward posters.

The trial was a prolonged complicated event because of the high- end lawyers provided by the Dutch investors. The main prosecuting witnesses were Lila and Wilbur Stannish,

Marshal Harrison, Mortimer Butler, Stanley Caruthers and several of the murdered claim owner's heirs. The multiple verdicts were the same, guilty as charged. VanHouten received a 20-year prison sentence. Two of the TDSM regulators were hung and two received 20-year prison sentences. Wilbur Stannish was named acting TDSM manager. The ventilating furnace was ordered to be completed. VanHouten had no family and his stock shares were confiscated by the state. The shares were bought by the TDSM investors. The living and heirs of the small claims were offered a very lucrative price for their claim which included a large cash payment and a percentage of the mining profits for the next twenty years.

Finally, after weeks of being away from home and their loved ones, the Trio of US Marshals was on their way back to New Braunfels.

***

CHAPTER 8

DIVISION OF DUTIES

During the trial, Sheriff Bixby came to speak to Rocky. "Myra Gunther has overheard Grant Galvin and his hired gun, Colonel Strickner, talk about burning down the Harrison ranch house during the middle of the night, and soon."

Rocky spoke, "I have five Apache braves watching house day and night. In that case, I double my braves to ten during nighttime, and I be the night watchman. We protect the house and boss' Missus."

"Be careful, these are killers. This is probably a case of kill or be killed."

"We try to scare them away, when they start shooting, we shoot to kill. Thank you for warning."

After the sheriff left, Red Flower and Rocky took some tools and a new bell ringer made by the blacksmith, and walked to the ranch house. "Missus Hannah, we make changes to the bell so you can ring it without going outside."

"Finally, you're calling me by my given name. Go ahead."

Rocky drills a hole in the kitchen wall as Red Flower attaches the ringer, secures a rope to it, and thru the kitchen wall. "There, all you have to do to call men in bunkhouse is to pull rope, heh, as you say!"

That night, Rocky climbed the pine tree next to the front door and told his braves to come out of hiding when they hear a double owl hoot call. The Apache braves had dug a trench to hide in and were covered with brush and grass.

As expected, around midnight, five riders came into the yard while quietly walking their horses. The leader says, "pour the kerosene on the front and back porch." At the same time, Rocky lets go a double owl hoot screech. The ten braves came out of their graves and started shooting arrows.

Rocky put an arrow in the man carrying two cans of kerosene. "Ouch, I've been shot, it's an arrow, INDIANS!" The arrows were flying, and the attackers all got arrows in arms, legs, and shoulders. Their horses were rearing up and dumping the wounded to the ground. At the same time, Red Flower had heard the owl hoot screech and ran to the kitchen to pull the rope. The bell rang out repeatedly and Hannah jumped out of bed in a total panic. Red Flower rushed in the bedroom and brought Hannah to her office to hide under her huge desk.

The leader said, "what in hell is that, a bell! Shoot the Indians before the bunkhouse wakes up." "Where are they, we can't see them." "Shoot anywhere and let's get out of here. The lights are on in the bunkhouse."

With gunshots, the Indians aimed for the chest and abdomen. Two men fell with arrows to the heart. The cowhands were running to the melee with shotguns and two more raiders went down. The leader saw he was alone and bolted away at a full gallop.

Once the leader was on the road, he never saw Clayton hiding by the road behind a tree. As he went by, Clayton let go both barrels and knocked the rider clear off his horse. Clayton later remembered the leader's appearance—white faced in a state of shock with arrows in his left thigh and shoulder.

Rocky then checked the downed men. One man was alive with multiple buckshot wounds to the belly. "You're dying mister, do right thing, and tell who put you up to this."

"It was Grant Galvin. We were supposed to set the place on fire and get out before anyone got shot. How did you know we were coming and where did those Indians come from" . . . . .as he took his last breath.

The next morning, Sheriff Bixby showed up with the undertaker. When he heard about the outlaw's dying statement, he agreed to relate this information to Judge Hobart along with Myra's signed affidavit of hearing Galvin's plans.

***

At noon Jake arrived. Walking in the house, he kissed Hannah and asked her what was new, why was there a kerosene puddle in the yard and why was there a rope hanging from the kitchen wall. Hannah answered, "Not much really. Let's see, Camilla, Sandra and Josie are pregnant and we're all due around Christmas, I sent two chapters to Isabella, I have three chapters to go, I need your synopsis of the mining caper to continue writing, Red Flower saved my life, Rocky with his braves saved our ranch house from burning, and they killed the five raiders sent by Galvin, your second oil well came in and Greg Webb is in love and wants to talk about working for us, the calving season is in full swing, Clayton is having a drive thru implement shed constructed, he has hired a mechanic to maintain and repair the agricultural implements, and he wants to talk to you about setting up an irrigation system to protect our herd and crops in case of a drought. Otherwise, THINGS WERE RATHER QUIET AND BORING."

"Great balls of fire, I only left for ten days. Guess I'm not needed anymore."

"That is wrong, you'll always be needed. This is proof of excellent division of duties and delegation of control. Now you need to have four sit downs; Judge Hobart to decide what to do with Galvin, Clayton for a follow up on crop cultivation, shed construction, fencing, calving and irrigation, Greg to take over the oil business and me to hear about your mining caper and my loving."

"Wow, you're not just the business accountant, but you have become my secretary. So, in order of importance, let's take care of loving first."

"In broad daylight, have you no shame?"

"Absolutely not, put the do not disturb sign out, and let's catch up on the lost ten days."

It was seemingly a short afternoon but after four hours, the duo decided they needed a replenishing supper and some personal time to discuss the mining caper before the business meetings in the morning.

***

Jake's first sit down was with Greg Webb. "Now that the well is in, I need a working manager who knows the oil industry and can take control of my oil enterprise. What are your credentials and your plans?"

"Starting with my background, I was raised in a small town outside of Dallas. After 10th grade, I spent a year in a Denver college studying the oil industry. I had practical experience drilling and extensive marketing preparations. My first job was drilling for oil for the Peabodys. Within a year, I became their foreman and got involved with negotiations with private distilleries. I was planning to return to Denver with the Peabodys until a certain gal came into my life."

"And who is this gal?"

"When I was negotiating your receiving station at the railroad yard, I had several dealings with the yard manager's secretary, Donna Silvers. We started stepping out and then courting and now she has said yes to my proposal. She has a large family in town and nearby ranches and with a great job, she would prefer to stay in New Braunfels but will move to wherever I find work."

"Well, the Peabodys both give you a high recommendation and apparently my wife has met Donna and has high praise to report, so let me make you an offer. I am prepared to offer you a salary of $100 per month and give you free housing. I will build you a ranch house/ barn between Clayton and Willie to utilize the same water well and will also include two riding horses/hay/oats. This allows you to be close to the oil wells and I believe the lady's comradery with Hannah, Erna, Josie, Camilla, Sandra and Laura will be good for Donna. She'll never feel alone even when you need to be out of town on business."

"Sir, that is a most generous offer, especially to include housing and horses. Donna presently lives at home in the countryside and rides her horse five miles to work every day. Living here will cut her traveling in half. I'm certain she will be jumping with joy with this offer. I gladly accept your offer but request that I finalize this offer with Donna."

"Done, assuming that it's a go, take a spot in the bunkhouse while we get Cass to build your new home. I'll want you and Donna to meet with Cecil Cass to get your personal input before he starts building. And Hannah and I want an invite to your wedding. Welcome aboard."

***

That afternoon, the Duo went to town. Hannah had her writing class and Jake met with prosecutor Cain Bishop and Judge Hobart. "We now have two events with signed affidavits that Galvin ordered the bank robbery and now the burning of your home. We cannot ignore this any longer. I am issuing an arrest warrant with charges of ordering property damage, endangering human lives, bank robbery with death resulting and wanton disregard to cease and desist."

"Galvin is still in the hospital; I'll have the

Deputy Marshals pick him up as soon as Doc Craven releases him."

Cain brought up Galvin's medical condition. "Before we get to a trial, be warned that the defense attorney will certainly bring up the beating you gave him. How are you prepared to defend your actions?"

"I was serving Judge Hobart's process to deliver a 'cease and desist' order. In Galvin's response, he threatened to kill me and my wife. At that point, being this was a threat against two US Marshals, I had two choices. One, to again arrest him, to answer to his threats, or give him the unwitnessed trouncing that this prick of misery deserved."

"Yes, that will certainly work for me. We're all set Judge."

After picking up Hannah, they went to Natalie's Diner for supper. Walt was having a private meal with Natalie. The Duo gave them the privacy they deserved. Their meal was the special of the day, chicken dumplings with mashed potatoes and peas. They then went to see the Wolfgangs. Herman mentioned that the benefactor account was down to $300 and Jake said he would deposit another $1,500 the next time he was in the bank. When asked how the egg deliveries were going, Helga had nothing but praise for the Newmanns and their delivery gal, Yvonne Washington. The social visit included talk of the oil wells, the changes on the ranch, Hannah's finding a book publisher and of course the expectant mother to be. Helga was pouring tears of joy and pride in her favorite undeclared daughter while Herman was shaking Jake's arm off.

That evening, they had undisturbed personal time in front of a sizzling fire. Hannah was studying her class textbook while Jake was totally absorbed in Hannah's business ledger. To his surprise, the ledger was separated in five sections; crop-cattle-oil-egg-lawman. Every expense was entered with a separate column showing a bill sequential number. Any income over $10 had a similar number to refer to the appropriate transaction. Income less than $10 was entered in petty cash. Each ledger section had its own set of employees. Anyone reading the ledger would have total understanding where money was going and where it was coming from. When Jake finished with the ledger, he quietly closed it and softly said, "nice job woman." Hannah heard him, smiled, and said nothing.

The next morning during a replenishing breakfast, Jake and Hannah were interrupted by Bromley Freighting. There were four men to deliver a heavy fireproof safe to hold the payroll and other monies. The safe was placed in the front office after the floor was reinforced. After the delivery, Clayton arrived.

"First of all, remember the safe's combination. The three of us are the only ones who know it. The only requirement is that when any of us make a withdrawal or deposit that we mark the amount in the tablet located in the safe. That way Hannah will mark that amount in her ledger."

"Now let's start with the new blacksmith. How is he working out?"

"I couldn't be any happier. Every riding and work horse has been reshod. Every set of shoes has been duplicated and labeled for each horse. Now when a horse loses a shoe, Rocky has a replacement and the horse is not out of commission. Stan has reinforced every wagon we have with steel angles and repaired many implements. We now have replacement wheels for every wheeled implement or wagon. He has also fabricated several parts needed on the oil rigs. He is basically the jack of all trades when it comes to working iron. He is finally accepting a standard wage and will continue working two days a week."

"Boy, that is good news. Also, his wife Yvonne, has good standing with the Wolfgang Mercantile. Hannah, please check with the Newmanns about how she is working out, and if everything is good, make sure she is being paid a decent wage for her time. It appears that these two were good additions. Now tell me about the fencing project."

"Every acre you own is surrounded by fence posts and half of those have three strands of barbwire. Your crop lands are all enclosed with four strands and that area has been increased to 1,000 acres—or ten 100-acre plots. The temporary fencing team will be involved with the harvest except for three of the older men who will continue adding wire.

By next winter, the project will be done."

"Excellent. Now why did you include 1,000 acres for crop lands?"

"I'll clarify that later."

"Ok, Hannah tells me you hired a mechanic. Tell me about this."

"The cropboys kept saying that they needed someone to take care of the implements since it took too much of their time away from crop work. So, I agreed and had the chance to find someone in town. The first thing he suggested was to get all our implements under cover. Since these are all powered by horses, a drive thru system was designed where every bay holds one or two implements and the horses simply drive thru to get unhitched. In the long run, it will pay off and allow the mechanic to work on repairs during the nights under kerosene lamps. That way the implement will be back online in the morning."

"Sounds like a wise decision. You do realize that this was the first big expense you authorized while I was gone."

"Well, not quite so. I didn't feel comfortable, so I bounced it off Hannah and well, the shed is now completed and housing all our implements. Had Hannah not been here, I would have given it the go ahead."

"Hannah tells me the calving season is upon us. Tell me how that is going and what % are the calves crossbreeds?"

"The boys have managed to herd the near-term cows into four areas surrounding a water source. They are watching these four areas day and night. They all have these new stainless-steel chains to help pull out calves. The older cowhands are teaching the young cowboys how to pull out a stuck leg or even turn a calf coming out sideways. Since half the season is over, it's very clear that the cows and first calf heifers are delivering the calves with a lot less complications than last year. In addition, the calves are much livelier, better at nursing and will be ready for branding/horn burning/ castration within a month."

"Now as far as the ratio, it appears that 90 percent of the calves are crossbreeds and seemed evenly distributed between bulls and heifers. We are now at the halfway point and it looks like we're going to end up with close to 700 new calves. Those Hereford and Durham bulls had a high insemination rate and even some unplanned young heifers got bred which accounts for the high yield. Those Longhorn bulls were not very active compared to the pure-bred Herefords and Durhams. We'll be able to give you a final tally later on, and we'll talk again before we start the roundup."

"Will do, and finally let's talk about the crops and this new issue about irrigation."

"As of this day, the cropboys are ready for planting. We have 400 acres of old land that has been fertilized with either horse manure, chicken manure or commercial phosphate. We have 300 new acres, fertilized with horse manure, that we'll plant with 100 acres of alfalfa and 200 acres of new hay. This summer we'll cultivate 100 acres for oats."

"I never even imagined that the cropboys could get so many acres cultivated and fertilized. You're talking of 800 acres that will yield some 1,500 tons of sellable or usable crops. That's close to $29,000."

"Yes, and a lot of work. Assuming there is no drought!"

"Drought, what drought are you talking about. A totally ruined crop would be catastrophic. Where are you heading with this?"

"Last year, there was a snow catastrophe in northern Texas that boosted the hay market. We live in south Texas where droughts are known to happen. A drought would mean no crop to sell and many animals dying from lack of water. We have too much invested to not take precautions against natural climate disasters that would bankrupt you."

"Agree, what do you propose? I don't know of any insurance companies that would protect against such losses."

"You're right. So, I had a long meeting with

our state and county agricultural agent by the name of Irving Galloway. The ag department is aware that the local economy would collapse with a drought. In response, there are county funds to help pay for an irrigation project that could save this ranch. The agent pointed out that the water for this ranch comes from three small rivers north of your property. The origin of the water is from mountain snow runoff, natural springs, and confluence of rivulets common in south Texas."

"We're interested, how does it work, what is involved and how much would it cost?"

"It involves the diversion of rivers, construction of dug out holding ponds/dams with side tanks for watering cows. The crop fields would be flooded thru a piping system, ditches and berms. Here are the master blueprints that covers the three rivers and the 1,000 acres I had fenced in."

The Duo started looking at the several pages of blueprints and turned the pages to examine all the details. Hannah finally said, "this is amazing, and you accomplished all this in ten days."

"No, Irving and I have been working on this for the past month. So far, the prep work and prints have cost you $250. Now the agent says that this entire project would be done by state contractors and the total bill would be $5,000 but the county would contribute $1,000 toward the project. I've thought about this for a long time and I think it is worth the one-time investment to guarantee a crop and the health of the herd."

Jake looked at Hannah and got that nod again, "why take the county's money, we can pay to get this done. I would prefer not to get in bed with state or county agencies."

"Normally, I would agree with you, but in this case, you need the liability protection of the state and the benefit of state contractors. You would be diverting rivers, damming ponds and controlling the water flow south of your land. This can only legally be done if it's part of a master government plan for the good of all. In this particular case, the land south of you is barren rocky land that has poor to no access. An absence of water in this aberrant land has no significance."

"When will this project start and how long will it take to complete?"

"It takes a $4,000 bank draft, signing this here contract, and the bulldozers will be here to start in three days. They will be done by early August with irrigation pipes to cover the 600 acres. That's just in time to save the second crop, which is when south Texas usually experiences the effect of a summer drought."

"Very good and well-done Clayton. We'll sign the contract and you can sign the bank draft. Let's get started ASAP. This is an excellent idea and good planning on your part."

***

The next day, Tommy arrived with a message from Judge Hobart. The message simply said, "issue in Austin, again." Jake decided to pay the Judge a visit and get more information.

Arriving at the courthouse, Jake stepped in the jail first. Walt was having a meeting with a new face wearing a jailer's badge. "Well Walt, is this your new jailer?"

"Yes, this is Phineas McGalloway. He's a retired deputy sheriff from Galveston who has moved into town to live near his grandchildren. His daughter is married to the gun shop owner, Barney Blackwell. He'll be taking over as jailer when I'm gone with the squad."

"Well, better get him ready, we'll be taking the train today, and you're coming along. I see the only prisoner is Galvin."

"Yes, but he's angrier than a two-peckered owl!"

"I don't know if that's the right association of words, but I understand what you mean."

Stepping upstairs, he knocked at Judge Hobart's office door. "Come in Jake. Marshal Grandville has another dilemma and he needs help."

"I hope it's not more cleaning out of winter outlaws!"

"No, this is even more serious. He has a ten-member outlaw gang that have taken residence around Austin. They have robbed three banks so far and there are still another nine banks, three credit unions and three mortgage lending institutions. They seem to hit that city every two weeks, which allows the citizens uproar to settle down and the posses to give up. They are expecting a hit within a week."

"Why hasn't Marshal Grandville put a stop to this gang?"

"Because of their MO. During the robbery, they send three men to shoot at the marshal's office. Two in the front and one out back. That keeps the lawmen pinned down till the gang escapes. Along with robbing the bank, the gang's leader, Grizz Slaughter manages to shoot someone dead every time—usually for no reason. The banks are running scared and are pushing Marshal Grandville to seek out help. The last time you were there, you impressed everyone with your squad's ability and determination. Any question why they're asking for you?"

"I see. Has Marshal Grandville tried to track them down and locate their camp?"

"Yes, apparently a gang member is sent to

town on a regular schedule to get meat, dry goods and whiskey. He always goes to Simmons Mercantile which is next door to a butcher. The Marshal and his deputies have tried to follow this man, but always lose him once the trail goes over a two-mile-wide rock ledge. The Marshal is hoping that Rocky can track him over this rock ledge."

"Very good, my entire squad, minus Hannah, will be on the train this afternoon and we'll do our best to solve the Marshal's problem. It seems to me that I have to find a way to disable this outfit, otherwise we'll be dealing with an outright gunfight confrontation with many dead men. That would also include somc dead squad members which is not acceptable."

Arriving in Austin in mid-afternoon, they all went to visit with Marshal Grandville and his deputies. There was little else to add to Judge Hobart's summary. After leaving, Jake sent his men to get hotel rooms and stable their horses as close to Simmons Mercantile as possible. They would then meet at the hotel restaurant for supper.

On his way to Simmons, Jake made a stop at an apothecary shop to pick up two containers of very specific veterinary medicines. Entering Simmons store, Jake introduced himself. Afterwards, he explained how he wanted to disable the Slaughter gang that was ravaging the local banks. When Simmons was asked if he would be willing to help him, he answered, "Heck yes, what do you want me to do?"

"When the suspected outlaw comes to get whiskey, how many bottles does he get?" "A case of twelve quarts."

"Fine, would you pour three ounces out of each bottle, add two ounces of this liquid and one ounce of this liquid and close the bottle back up."

Simmons looks more carefully at Jake's two bottles and reads, "concentrate of syrup of ipecac and super concentrated phenolphthalein. Simmons breaks out in laughter and adds, "that should bring an elephant down on its knees." "Not exactly what I'm after, but it should disable those outlaws, heh?" "Oh yeah! Assuming you can track this outlaw, you'll have a hell of a show when you get to their camp."

"By the way, can you give us any distinguishing horse markings to help spot this hombre? I'll be spending the days to come across the street in front of the barbershop."

"Yes, his packhorse is a pinto with skew-bald markings of white and brown patches. Kind of stupid for an outlaw to have a 'marked horse.'"

"Yes, but helpful to the lawmen."

The next morning, in case the outlaw had decided to visit another mercantile, each squad member was assigned his own mercantile to watch. The rule of engagement was to let him leave, and then start gathering the remainder of the squad for the tracking. Jake only hoped this outlaw would come back to Simmons to get the "hot hooch."

Hours passed when suddenly around 1PM the outlaw arrived with his skew-bald pinto packhorse. Jake watched and true to form, the outlaw went to get several packages at the butcher shop and then entered Simmons store. Eventually, he had a case of whiskey which he put in the second basket, and plenty of vittles tied in burlap bags that were draped over the packsaddle. Without any suspicion or apparent care, he just slowly rode his horse/packhorse out of town.

Jake then went to gather his squad. They saddled their horses, loaded their rifles and shotguns, picked some cold and hot camp vittles, added winter coats for cold spring nights, and started tracking their prey.

***

The tracks out of town and along the road were easy for all to follow at a medium trot. When the rider turned cross-country Rocky changed to a very slow trot and the squad followed. Then everyone suddenly found themselves on solid rock and all came to a complete stop. Rocky gave his horse's reins to Jake and started to look carefully at the rock surface. His only words were, "this be a challenge."

Rocky had his nose to the rock. He was looking for scratches, disturbed pebbles, crushed solitary plants growing in cracks, smelling the rock for urine, checking the temperature and consistency of horse manure, disturbed dirt or moss, fallen trappings from hoofs, and many other signs that had no significance to the observing squad. The boys were impressed when Rocky was seen touching a wet spot and tasting the tip of his finger for second time. Willie asked him, "what does that tell you?" "Man smokes a quirley, now twice I taste it, we on right tract."

Rocky earned every inch, and after two long hours, was certain that the new tracks beyond the rock ledge were the same as the ones out of town. They followed him at a slow walk until they smelled camp smoke. They then hitched their horses on long tethers to allow them to feed and walked with the tracks toward the smoke smell. At 100 yards, the camp was well seen thru their 50X binoculars. Jake told them to choose a hiding spot and wait for the show. When Walt asked what to expect, Jake said, "I had that case of whiskey laced with something to make them throw up and have the backdoor trots."

"I guess I still don't understand, what is the big deal about having a sour stomach and maybe some diarrhea." Furman looked at Walt and said, "I don't think that's all Jake had in mind. Now fess up Jake!"

"Well after they lose lunch, they'll retch for an hour while the explosive dumps will bring goose bumps to your skin. I gave them a colic relieving horse purgative. In a horse it's a mild laxative, but in a man, the explosive expulsions will lift any man off a privy seat."

The squad waited while the outlaws were drinking away and creating a ruckus. Then one man said, "damn, I don't feel so good and proceeded to have a propulsive vomitus hit another man in the face. The others laughed but suddenly were trying to drop their drawers. Some did not get to open their union-suit back-door when the sudden call of nature filled their suit and britches. Others started to throw up, and the retching compounded the explosive diarrhea. After a half hour of torture, the outlaws were getting weak. Jake decided to wait till the diarrhea stopped when each man would be getting dehydrated and would not be in any shape to start shooting.

When the squad approached the camp, Rocky was first to say something. "White man was full of sheeeeet. Now stinks, next time we shoot it out instead of ruining sense of smell." The boys stood a bit away from the liquid soupy excrement. Jake said, "give them all a half canteen of water to help getting rid of the poison." Mad Dog lifted his head and said, "you miserable lawman, you poisoned us, I'm going to kill you for this." Jake added, don't touch your pistol or I'll put you down." Mad Dog face changed to raw anger as he went for his gun. Jake pulled both triggers on his sawed-off shotgun and blew the outlaw down the soupy mess. The remainder of the outlaws had no fight left and took the water as ordered.

The water did its trick. It cleared the intestines of any residual purgative, but it also restarted the explosive expulsions in the process.

When the cleansing was finished, the outlaws were stripped of clothing and herded to the stream with a bar of lye soap. While the scrubbing went on the squad picked up their belongings that were not contaminated with the soup and moved the camp a hundred yards away. The outlaws were then redressed with whatever clean clothing could be found and then were manacled to their own tree for the night.

The squad started a new campfire, used the outlaws' vittles, and cooked a full supper of ham, fresh eggs, canned beans, canned beef stew, fresh biscuits and plenty of coffee. They had their fill and never offered a morsel to the outlaws.

One outlaw yelled out, "hey we're pretty weak and thirsty, how about some food and water." "Nope, no leftovers and no water to spare."

"Well, it's going to be cold tonight, how about some jackets or blankets." "Nope, none to spare, no extras."

"Why you miserable punks, I'll kill some of you before we get to Austin."

That did it, Jake got up and with a stick of firewood rearranged that loud-mouth's face.

"The next time you open your mouth, I'll send the Indian back here and he'll cut your tally-wacker off."

The night was cold, but the squad was comfortable in their winter coats while the outlaws shivered all night. In the morning, the saddlebags were emptied of the stolen loot and some $14,000 was collected. Since $13,000 had been stolen from three banks, the squad divided the balance. The guns and valuables were collected for future sales. After the squad had their breakfast, they helped the manacled outlaws onto their horses, then secured one ankle to the stirrup and started riding back to town with the dead Mad Dog stretched over the saddle.

Marshal Grandville greeted the marshals and took over the prisoners. They would be identified, and any reward would be wired by Western Union to New Braunfels. The local banks would share the $13,000 in collected loot. The guns and horses would be sold, and the funds sent to Captain Ennis. The district judge would take care of the trial and US Marshals would return only if required by the prosecutor.

The squad had the luck to be on time for the late train going home and would arrive by supper time. While traveling, Jake wondered what else could have happened at home, in just a week's time. Jake realized that, although he had delegated many duties, his plate was still spilling over. Maybe it was time to unload something and keep what he enjoyed the most. He wondered what Hannah would say on the subject?"

***

The squad arrived home unexpectedly. Hannah was pleased to no end. Jake had barely said hello when Hannah jumped in his arms and covered him with a passionate kiss. "Hey, I've only been gone a week and you act as if I've been gone a month."

"Husband, I miss you every day and night when you're gone." Jake pondered and realized what it was in life that he enjoyed the most, being with his wife."

"I'll show you how much I missed you later tonight, for now, tell me what is new?"

"Clayton has been busy as usual and he wants a sit-down tomorrow morning after our replenishing breakfast, heh? For now, sit down, I have a subject I want to discuss with you."

"Go ahead, you have my undivided attention."

"I've been thinking about this burning off of calves' horn buds. I think it is unwise. You are trying to start a new breed of cattle. By breeding the Texas Longhorns with purebred Hereford and Short Horn bulls, the offsprings will automatically have horns about half the length of the Longhorns. That will identify them as a new breed. A polled crossbreed herd is not natural."

"You have a good point; we'll think this over."

"There are other reasons the vet brought up. If you burn horn buds, you have to delay the roundup for the buds to be ready. That will bring the roundup right in the harvest season. And we can't have that with the 700 acres you want to harvest early to give us a second crop. That would be a financial conundrum."

"I see, any other reason?"

"As the vet said, some of the burnt buds will bleed and delay the calf's growth. Or worse, some will get infected and we will lose some calves. Besides, as a woman, I think it is downright cruel. Now as it stands, the roundup can start in two weeks for branding and castration and we'll be done before the first crop harvest. All around, burning horn buds is definitely a poor financial move! And that's all I will say on the subject, I know you'll make the right decision since you do your best work when you're on top of things. No pun intended!"

"Wow, that was a hell of a chin-wag. It appears you are quite bitten by the ranch's goings on?"

"What do you mean?"

"Looking back, you started as a chicken farmer, then became a writer, then joined the marshal squad, then became the accountant, and finally you've become a business financial advisor."

"I don't mean to obfuscate you, but yeah, I guess so. This enterprise has become simply addicting. And, most importantly, it is something we can do together as a couple and soon as a family."

"What about your writing, total involvement with the business will become an interference, won't it?"

"I have thought about this, we'll move my office with yours and I'll type when there is nothing going on. My office will become the nursery which will be accessible from the front office and our bedroom by adding adjoining doors. My writing will change after this book is done. I am writing this type of fiction since my advisor pushed me to write about what I knew. I don't want my future books to be labeled a 'parody' and I'll develop my own story without using your bounty hunter and marshal capers."

"What is a parody?"

"Imitating other writers and adding a comical twist. If you think back, I read your four bounty hunter books by Swanson, Harnell, Adams and McWain. Along with their style, I added some comical twist like the wang leather sting and others. Well, I already know how my style will change. But writing will be my hobby. That being something I enjoy and can do any day. The business will be my first concern."

Jake was stunned and finally spoke, "how did I ever find you?"

"Actually nude, draped over a rock, exposing my female attributes and held there by two heartless animals while waiting to be raped."

"All women have female attributes; it was your brain and your heart that made me fall in love with the greatest woman on earth. I also miss being with you and I had an epiphany after this last marshal caper. It is time for me to make a change. Being a lawman takes a man away from his family, his business, and the wife never knows if her husband will return. Living by the gun will eventually be fatal."

"Whoa, you spent your life training for this profession, and you had made it your destiny. Are you sure, are you reacting to my change in values?"

"I agree that it appeared to be my destiny, but

now I know that it was a 'transitional destiny.' My future is here, on this ranch, and with you. I have no doubts and will notify Judge Hobart on my next and final caper. I will recommend that Furman become the head marshal."

"Well, let's have supper and then you can make your final decision in the morning after sleeping on it."

"Heck, romping in the bed with you is not going to change my mind, woman! I don't plan, after a long week, to get much sleep!"

"Is that a hint that you want to skip supper?"

"No, we'll need the energy to get us by, till our replenishing breakfast, heh?"

***

CHAPTER 9

DESTINY

The next morning, after a replenishing breakfast of scrambled eggs, home fries, bangers and coffee, Clayton arrived with his clip-board.

"Have some coffee and Hannah tells me you have been stirring the pot again. I'm eager to hear what is new."

"Well, we've been getting ready for the harvest. The mechanic has been repairing and maintaining our implements. He has sharpened the mower blades and the baler knives. He's serviced all the implements, changed worn out drive chains, and reinforced the wagons. All axles have been greased and a whole lot of other preparatory chores done. We got ourselves a good man and he works well with our blacksmith."

"The first crop will be a good one. There was plenty of rain in April and May. Now the fields have dried up because it has not rained since June 1st. The county agent has been pushing the contractors since he suspects that weather parameters are predicting a drought. He has the three retention ponds finished, has diverted the streams, and they are all filling up. The contractors are busy building ditches and laying pipes for flooding the fields by the second crop. If he is right, the drought will hit our area hard and the local ranchers will be relying on our hay to get thru the next winter. So, Hannah, please don't send out contracts to our buyers in Dallas till we know whether our ranchers will need our help."

"As far as planning goes, we needed a fourth baler, which will arrive in a week. Baling is the one step that slows down processing the hay. As is, we'll be baling 24 hours a day, and yes, under the kerosene lamps. Red Flower has been training extra horses, to walk the cam around, to power the balers. The horses will be rotated every four hours. Rocky will now help her with the task and the horses will be ready."

The major reason for this meeting is the results of the calving season. First, we lost 8 calves that the vet believes were genetic deformities and recommends we bring these 8 older cows to market. Now, I thought we might give them to the Indians, who just spent the last week, working 24 hours a day guarding the house and Hannah. Would you agree to giving these 8 beefers to Rocky's family in the reservation?" "Of course, have the boys drive them there before the roundup." Hannah adds, "that's a nice touch, Clayton!"

"Great, now before we discuss the calving statistics, we need to ride to one of four birthing herds to show you the results of our first crossbreeding attempt. The Trio saddled their horses and headed for the range. Arriving, they noted several cowboys riding amidst the herd. "The newborn calves are susceptible to coyotes in the first two weeks and cowhands will babysit the herd day and night till roundup. Now look at the calves. The Hereford crossbreeds have red spots mixed with the Longhorn multi colors. The Durham crossbreeds have a mixture of brown with the Longhorn colors. The crossbreeds, as a result of breeding a Longhorn with one of those crossbreed bulls, are not quite as apparent but are certainly different than the purebred Longhorn calves. So, this is what I wanted you to see, but what is missing?"

Hannah recognized the deficiency and said, "there is no black colored calves!" "That is absolutely correct. How do we resolve this issue?"

Jake knew the answer, "wc need some purebred Black Angus bulls and heifers. I will send a telegram to Emmett Powell at the Circle P Ranch in San Antonio where we got the Hereford and Durham bulls and heifers. He had some Black Angus on order from Scotland, and I had asked him to try to get some for me as well. It would be nice to have bulls and heifers for the early summer breeding season."

Getting back to the ranch, Clayton took

over the discussion. "So far we have 679 healthy appearing calves. The birthing was clearly less traumatic with these crossbreed calves and the cows are all doing well. The breakdown is:

Purebred Herefords 20

Purebred Durham Short Horn 20

Purebred Longhorn 19

Longhorn + Hereford ....+- 215(1st gen. crossbreed)

Longhorn + Durham Short Horn .... +- 220(1st gen. crossbreed)

Longhorn + Crossbreed...........+- 185(2nd gen. crossbreed)

"The 19 purebred Longhorn calves was the result of having purebred Longhorn bulls in the herd until we smartened up and pulled them out. So, castrate the Longhorn bulls and, at the fall show, I'll use them to compare their growth against crossbreed steers. The heifers will eventually be bred for crossbreeding."

"Now there will not be any burning of horn buds." Hannah interrupted, "Jake and I have already discussed the reasons."

"For the fall show, I need six castrated bulls of each of the three crossbreed categories. Don't castrate any other bull, purebred or crossbreed. These will be our future stock to promote crossbreeding."

"When the breeding season begins, I would like you to separate the purebred Hereford and Durham cows into their own paddock with their own purebred bulls like we did last season. This is the only way I can producc purebred animals. Eventually, segregation will end, and the purebred heifers will be bred by other bulls to continue crossbreeding."

Clayton added, "At this rate, in five years, we'll have a 100% crossbred herd and the Longhorns will have all gone to market. What will we call this herd since they will now be their own entity?" Hannah answered, "then they will be called 'Crossbreeds.'"

Clayton agreed. “Now we have an issue of identifying these first- and second-generation crossbreeds from second- and third-generation crossbreeds next year and every year thereafter.”

Jake adds, “should we have a different brand each year?”

“No, by law we cannot change the brand by the year. The brand is for identification of ownership. It is not for identifying generations or specific individual characteristics. We need something different, and it cannot be just for the generation. We need to identify every animal by a unique number, and that’s calf and cow and all our bulls/steers.”

Both Hannah and Jake said in unison, “how in blazes do we do that, we have 679 calves this year alone and more next year, and you want to include the entire herd as well. That’s impossible.”

“No, it is possible with the use of ear tags. These are tin or aluminum with clear black numbers from 1 to 5000. They are attached from the bottom of the right ear with a pin that perforates the ear lobe and is applied by a quick single squeeze of special pliers. Now let me list the benefits of identifying ear tag numbers.

- Separation of the six different classes just mentioned.
- Labeling cows with birthing difficulties.
- Selecting animals that need recurring hoof trimming.
- Barren cows are identified for culling.
- Labeling a troublemaker for culling.
- Labeling a fence jumper for culling.
- Identify a good active breeder.
- Identify aggressive dangerous bulls for culling.
- Select a leader with positive traits.
- Label any non-thriving animal.
- Identify cows whose calf did not survive for culling.

Hannah adds, "looks like, I'll be keeping a separate ledger to keep track of all these categories, but I think this is a fabulous idea." Jake adds, "I like it, I really like it. Now, how do we do this before the approaching harvest?"

"With expert and experienced help. The bad winter up north has devastated the ranchers who have had to let go many cowhands. There are eight in town who have hired on to secure the cows for tagging as is done up north. This will not interfere with the regular calf branding, castrating and ear tagging done by our cowhands."

"Well Clayton, this is a go with us. How long to get the ear tags to cover the herd?" "Uh, well, you told me to make decisions when you were gone, so I did this time. I already have tags from 1 to 5,000 with pins and a half dozen attaching pliers."

Jake adds, "huum, I guess so. You bought a new baler, hired 8 more cowboys and committed us to tagging all the cattle. All good choices, Clayton!"

***

After Clayton left, Hannah asks, "well, have you come to a final decision regarding your destiny."

"Yes. Before I say more, answer this one

question. "What made you change your mind so drastically from a month ago?"

"After being alone twice during your last assignments, I realized that I was not just lonely, but I needed to share my life with you from day to day. With a baby, I was never going to join you on your marshal assignments. This two-way profession was not going to be conducive to longevity. I found the man of my life and I want to be with you. My decision was easy. Now you have to make up your own mind."

"What you said last night about destiny really struck home. I agree that I trained for years to be a lawman and the result was a given. I accomplished reaching my first destiny and that was what I was meant and directed to be—at that time. Now that I have matured and found new interesting avenues and responsibilities, I feel that my destiny is changing."

Hannah adds, "our current status may again change in the future as we find that this current destiny may again be a transitional one. I guess change is part of life, heh?"

"For now, I plan to resign from the US

Marshal Service and will notify Judge Hobart of this at our next and last major assignment."

***

"Let's have some dinner, you have a meeting with Greg Webb at 1PM and I have my writing class this afternoon. I'll leave early and send that telegram to Emmett Powell. If we're lucky, there might be an answer by the end of my class."

"You're not going alone to town with Galvin still a threat, even if he's in the federal jail."

"I know, I have my Bulldog in my reticule, my pump shotgun at my side and Furman/ Willie as my bodyguards. Your wife and baby are well protected."

Greg arrived on time with his ledger. "The two wells are still at max production of 190 barrels a day. We've been fortunate to have contracts with four private distilleries and the demand has been high. The barrels are paying 75 cents each and we'll continue shipping as long as the price stays above 60 cents a barrel. Your 5,000 sq. ft. shed is ready and would hold

1,000 barrels. I know that is only five days of production, but the railroad is willing to rent boxcars that hold 100 barrels for $10 a month. That's not a bad deal, and we'll use this on a trial basis. Of course, these are the cars that will be first on the rails to fulfill an order."

"What are the oil moguls, experts, and pundits predicting for crude prices this summer?"

"All indicators are predicting $1 a barrel by winter. Heating fuel oil has gotten big in cities and will likely push the price up. Gasoline usage is going up all the time and that drives the price of crude up as well."

"What are the big oil companies doing and how are they affecting the private distilleries?"

"They are still hoarding their crude. They have their own distilleries and will not affect our buyers that much. However, when their crude comes on-line, they will flood the market and drive the barrel prices way down. So, time to make hay is when the sun shines. That is why we're shipping when the demand is high, and the prices hold up."

"Are you all set as far as equipment goes?"

"I've ordered two replacement pumps to transfer the crude to the railroad yard. I have duplicates of everything else since these parts are not common items at our local hardware stores. One of my workers is our mechanic as well, and he is capable of making repairs quickly to avoid much down time."

"How are you set for workers and what are you paying them?"

"We are running three shifts at each well and the receiving station. Each shift requires three men at the wells and four men at the receiving station. Roughly $10 per shift, or $30 a day or $900 a month plus my salary."

"It's not about money, we know it takes money to make money. We fully realize that 190 barrels a day at 60 cents generates $3,500 each month, so if you need more workers, hire the help you need because we cannot spare any cowhands or crop workers to help you out."

Hannah adds, "what we can offer you is to take over the bookkeeping and accounting. I will be taking over the entire ranch's accounting. I will have a separate ledger for the oil business.

I will pay your bills and receive payments for each crude delivery, and I'll be doing your banking and payroll as well. That will free you up to manage the oil business and all the contract negotiations with refineries. It is more important for you to keep orders 'coming and going' than to do paperwork."

"Wow, that is amazing. I agree with you that it is up to me to keep orders coming in and empty barrels coming back in a timely fashion. Some refineries just don't seem to understand that idle oil barrels are just an extra expense for the suppliers to keep expensive inventories."

"When I set up your ledger, are there any specific entries that I should plan on."

"Yes. Every boxcar of 100 barrels has an invoice which denotes the purchasing refinery. Every boxcar will eventually have a bank voucher sent as payment for that boxcar. That way you know where the shipments are going and where the money is comes from. This prevents the refineries from shuffling themselves out of paying for an occasional 100 barrels. Also, remember that we have a shipping fee for each boxcar of shipped crude, but the shipping charge for returning barrels is the distilleries' responsibility."

"Ok, this was a good meeting, we'll have more of these, since we both want to stay current with the every-day goings on." Before leaving, Greg handed the bills due, added a payroll schedule, the incoming income vouchers to match the outgoing invoices and a few other miscellaneous items to add to the ledger.

As Greg was stepping off the porch, Jake asked him if Donna might be interested in doing some part-time bookkeeping when Hannah's delivery time arrived. Greg answered, "in case you had not noticed, my wife is already tied to Hannah at the ankles. I'm certain that helping her out won't be an issue. Donna finally found some nice friends amongst the neighbors. It's such a pleasure to see her happy, and our new house doesn't diminish her happy mood. One day we'll find a way to repay your generosity. For now, all we can say is thank you."

Hannah then went to her writing class with her escort and a telegram to send. That evening, she returned with Powell's answer. Hannah simplified the telegram by saying, "the answer basically says to send a Western Union voucher for $1,200 to cover for 20 Black Angus bulls and $1,000 for 20 Black Angus heifers both ready for breeding this summer. The animals will be loaded tomorrow and will arrive in our train yard in two days. There was also mentioned, the fact that he would have purebred Hereford, Durham Short Horn, and crossbreed bulls for sale this fall, and asked if we would advertise this at our fall show."

***

The animals arrived on time and Clayton was there to receive them and drive them back to their new home. Clayton was enthralled to no end. He said, "this genetic addition of a black hide trait will complete our herd transformation. Now we're really going to have a true crossbreed herd."

The roundup started two weeks later. Each day, Jake would visit the current birthing site undergoing the roundup. Jake was especially impressed with the new cowhands' ability to restrain the full-size Longhorns for ear tagging. Jake noted that the six-week-old crossbreed calves were lively, energetic and thriving.

For the first time, Jake was able to outline the roundup setup. Two work zones were established. Each zone had their own fire to heat up the brands. Two cowhands were lassoing the calves and bringing them, with the cow following, to the receiving men. Two men were busy wrestling the calves to the ground as one man applied the brand, and another tagged the ear. During all this, four men were restraining the cow and tagging her ear. The cow and calf were released simultaneously, and the process was repeated. It was the man wielding the hot brand to enter the cow's and calf's ear number in the field ledger, and enter the calf's crossbreed class. Later the field ledger would be given to Hannah to copy. Clayton would keep the original field ledger for daily reference. Hannah would then set up each purebred and crossbreed class with the listed ear tag numbers.

The roundup lasted three weeks, and the

entire herd was ear tagged including the new Black Angus herd. The four birthing herds were now integrated, and the calves were hardy enough with their mothers to fight off coyotes. The cowhands took a few days off in anticipation of the harvest season about to start.

***

One evening after supper, Cain Bishop, the Federal and District prosecutor, arrived to see the duo. "I wonder if I could discuss an issue with you two?" "Of course, have a seat and some coffee. What's on your mind?"

"The Judge and I are considering a plea deal with Grant Galvin. To explain why this is being considered, Galvin has had a turnaround in his demeanor and attitude. After the thrashing you gave him, a 30-day stint in jail, and now facing a trial for causing a bank robbery, murder and attempted burning of your ranch house; he is amenable to a deal."

"The reason we are considering a deal is because of the flamboyant and aggressive lawyer he has hired to defend him. We are a bit leery to present the statements of prisoners who might have agreed to a lesser sentence turning state's evidence on the bank robbery case, and the words of a dying man, heard by an Indian. This man had been mortally wounded by Indians and was likely in a state of shock before he died. Plus, we fear we may take a hit on the thrashing you gave the man to put him in the hospital. Put all these factors into account, a local jury may vote to acquit him or be a hung jury."

"We can appreciate your hesitation. What is the deal or what is Galvin asking?"

"Galvin doesn't want a long prison sentence because his foreman, Kevin Wood, is predicting a drought that could wipe out his herd. He is asking that you sell his foreman hay to get his herd thru winter's poor forage season or he will have to sell the herd now at a huge loss."

"So, the man wants hay and a short sentence! What is the proposed sentence?"

"One year in Huntsville minus time served, a $5,000 restitution fee for the murdered victim's family, and civility with you and Hannah after he gets out of prison."

Jake looks at Hannah who gives him the nod. "Civility makes it for us and we'll keep his herd alive at the same rate we'll charge all the local ranchers. Go ahead and make the deal. This is good for everyone. We want to be on good terms with all our neighbors, and that includes Galvin." Hannah adds, "and thank you for seeing the long-term benefits for our community."

Cain had one final thought, "I'm the one who thanks you. Afterall, the man will be your neighbor and everyone needs to be at peace in the neighborhood. Oh, I almost forgot, Judge Hobart needs to see you tomorrow morning, if possible. He has intelligence of an impending attack on our town."

After Cain left, Jake says, "before I see the Judge, I need to talk to Furman. How would you like to ride along and make a visit to the Belchers before it gets dark?" "Are you sure, once you talk to Furman, the die will be cast?" "Yes, more determined than ever!"

***

"Good evening, what brings you this fine evening." "We have an issue to discuss with you and Laura. Where are the boys?"

"You don't know? The boys are working overtime to lay irrigation piping before they start the harvest." "No, that's Clayton's job."

"So, what's on your mind?"

"I've decided to retire from the Marshal Service. I guess I have several professions that I can follow, and I choose to be a rancher, oilman, crop-man, and a family man."

"Laura answered, "we're not surprised, and we knew that this day would come. You have a massive enterprise to manage and being a US Marshal needs your complete attention." Furman adds, "you made the wise choice. Good for you."

"That leaves a vacancy in the Marshal Service. Would you be interested in falling in my footsteps?"

"Laura and I have already broached the subject. We're in our 40's and we're finally making enough money to save for our retirement. I would be willing to take the lead if the Judge or Captain Ennis agrees."

"Very good, I'll be seeing the Judge tomorrow and will recommend you as my replacement. You'll need an extra deputy and Captain Ennis may have a veteran who wants to leave Colorado."

"Are the marshal's salary and benefits expected to remain the same?"

"Yes, and it includes sharing the reward bounties. The sale of the horses and guns goes to Captain Ennis. There had been some talk of converting the entire US Marshal Service to the Judge or to the Marshals, but that idea has been dropped. The Texas budget allowances keeps everything as is."

"Does this mean that you won't be available to help us in any situation?"

"I would never leave you in a lurch. If you ever need my help because of a dangerous assignment, you'll be able to count on me."

Laura sighed, "that was the one request I had. Thank you!"

***

The next morning, Jake headed to the courthouse. His first stop was the jail. "Good

morning Walt, how is your prisoner doing?"
"He's doing much better since Cain Bishop offered him the deal he wanted. Actually, he asked if you would come and see him before he was transferred to Huntsville."

"Really. Well, I'm here now, might as well get it over with."

Stepping in the cell block he says, "Mister Galvin, I hear you want to have a word with me. Before you say anything, let me say that I'm sorry for killing your son!"

"Thank you for saying that. Looking back, I now know that it was unavoidable. Any man would have done the same thing. You had no choice when my son went for his gun. In regard to my tax evasion, I was wrong to transfer my anger on life's frustrations onto you—you were just the messenger. As far as the bank robbery and the arson attempt, I guess I'll spend the rest of my life making it up to the community, the murdered victim's family and you. As far as my plea deal, I'm aware that it was approved because you and your wife agreed to it. You have to be one heck of a big man, despite everything

I threw at you, you have agreed to sell hay to my foreman and keep my life's work alive till I return."

"Stop. The past has gone by, shake my hand and we'll start over when you get out in a year. Meanwhile, I'll help Keith keep your ranch afloat and your cattle alive."

Stepping upstairs, Jake was waved into the Judge's office and found the sheriff already there. "Hello Marshal, have I got a problem to deal with!" "Stop right there, Judge, I have an announcement to make. After this assignment, I am retiring from the Marshal Service."

"I beg your pardon. . . . . .why?"

"Two reasons, dependents and the incvitable. When a lawman is single the only people who will be affected by his death are loving family and friends. When there are wives and children involved, it is not acceptable to make them live with the fact, when you live by the gun day to day, it's just a matter of time before you die by the gun. Hannah is with child, and I want to be with her to raise our children."

"I cannot argue the point, you have a sound

reason for changing your destiny especially with the empire you have developed. Do you have a name for a replacement as head Marshal?"

"Yes, I've talked with Furman, and he's willing to accept the position. He is experienced, has sound judgement, and will serve you well. He is completely trustworthy."

"I agree with you, actually all your men have strong work ethics and I can work with all of them, including Rocky, heh? I'll pass the message along to Captain Ennis and I'm sure he'll approve the change."

"Now, let me tell you why I called you to this meeting. Sheriff Bixby has a high school friend who works as a miner in the silver mines of San Saba north of San Antonio. This man sent a letter to the sheriff informing him of an outlaw army forming north of town. Their plan is to attack all four banks in town while crippling the sheriff and his deputies by keeping them under the siege of gunfire."

"The army is made up of three well known gangs that have escaped capture despite their depredations all over Texas. The separate gangs are led by Cletus Haltomire, Waldo Bendix and Homer Dooling. These are psychopathic murderers who are all wanted with large rewards. It appears that the mastermind behind this attack is Cletus himself. According to the wanted posters there can be as many as 16 outlaws in the gang."

"With that many men, this sounds like an invasion. Isn't this a job for the Texas Rangers?"

"Yes, it is, but when I requested their help, the answer came back that they were chasing a bunch of ruthless Comancheros marauding in the Rio Grande Valley. They have been gone a week without any communications back at the main office in McAllen. In short, the payroll deposits are arriving by train from Austin in three days and that is when the attack is likely to happen. We need to stop them before they arrive in town and create chaos. Sheriff Bixby will now give you his intelligence findings."

"Herman Wolfgang reported that a messenger arrived daily to pick up vittles and whisky for a large number of men. Knowing this info matched the intelligence from my friend, I decided to follow this man. Some ten miles north of here, I came to a tent city in the middle of a heavily forested area. A remuda was staked out next to a stream with good grass. I counted 21 horses, 17 men, 2 campfires, 8 individual tents, 4 large tents with lean-to's, and 2 utility wagons. I watched them till late and found they kept two rotating guards all night on a three-hour schedule. The guards would stay in the campsite and occasionally walk over to check on the horses but did not guard the horses continually."

"Wow, Herb, that's good intel. Can you say what these men do all day?"

"They play cards, eat and drink. It looks to me that the head man. Haltomier, won't let them leave camp and ruin the chance for a surprise attack. I heard several men try to convince him to let them go to town, but he refused. These arguments have led to several fist fights, but the guards keep the men in camp at gunpoint. It's my opinion that once the payroll monies arrive, it's going to take a real army to stop them."

"Sounds like you're right Herb, which means

we have to dwindle their numbers, disable as many as we can, scare some to desert, and cause a rift between gangs. We'll do all this by preventing them from leaving the camp and then we'll terrorize them mercilessly day after day till they become a useless gang of galoots."

"Herb, I assume you can lead us to their campsite so we can start playing with their heads as quick as today. I'll go gather my squad, vittles, and tools of my jungle warfare. I'll be back at your office in two hours."

As Jake was leaving, he heard Herb say to the Judge, "oh God, I've seen some of his jungle warfare. The disruption, demoralization and devastation will be worse than a tornado, and I'm going to get to see it all. Ha, Ha, Haah!"

Getting back at the ranch with Walt, Jake went thru his jungle tools and selected the ones that would fit this caper while Walt went to pick up Willie, Furman and Rocky. Hannah was anxious and tried to hide her fear. "Jake, this is an army you're going after. Are you sure you and your squad can handle this?"

"Of course, we can't, but my beartraps and

other contraptions will pulverize them. This will turn out to be one of our easiest assignments. We'll all be OK, so, stop worrying, heh? We'll be back in a week. Don't be surprised if the Apaches come back to protect you, since they don't know about the plea deal with Galvin."

"I know, Red Flower already told me she would be in for supper, spend the night, and has already sent a cowboy to inform her Indian family. I really enjoy and trust her with her new sawed-off shotgun."

They kissed and hugged. With two packhorses and a total of four panniers, the squad was on its way.

***

Sheriff Bixby had no difficulty to retrace his steps, and in three hours he had the squad hidden 200 yards from the outlaw encampment. The Marshals all spotted the camp with their 50X binoculars, and all agreed that the site seemed overpowering. It was Willie who said, "looking at the folderol these outlaws tag along, now I know how the Indians felt when they watched a military encampment. How in the heck are we going to get control of this bunch?"

"We're going to prevent them from leaving and terrorize them till they lose all desire to fight. And I'm going to start right now. Jake takes out his scoped Win 76, sets it on a tripod rest, and scans the camp. The outlaws were romping about without a care when Jake pulled the trigger and an outlaw was decapitated with a facial shot. The remainder took cover. Half an hour later, Jake spotted a large Dutch oven over the fire. He took aim and blew the cast iron pot to smithereens. Several of the outlaws were covered with stew. Jake waited another half hour when the outlaws figured the sniper had left. As they started to stand and walk about, Jake pulled the trigger and another man was thrown about. This time, the outlaw landed in the fire pit, started thrashing and screaming, as he finally went still when none of his buddies came over to pull him out of the fire.

Walt said, "man, if that don't start the reign of terror, nothing else will." Jake added, "no, there is plenty more coming." Furman adds, "two down and fifteen to go."

After midnight, the squad found the area that the outlaws were using for their natural calls. The area smelled terribly since nothing had been buried. The squad laid out a bear trap surrounded by several wolf traps and multiple anchored nails. After camouflaging them, most went back to their observation spot and waited. Rocky decided to climb a pine tree over the bushes to watch more closely the result of their trap's setups.

Around 3AM an outlaw got up, put his boots on and headed to the bushes. The entire squad heard a clear snap and a howl from hell followed. The outlaws all jumped up, without boots, and rushed to the sound of a trapped animal. When they found their friend, they naturally started to encircle him when the smaller wolf traps started going off. Men were falling to the ground and wailing away. What made it worse were the anchored nails. Several men stepped on them, and because they had rushed to the first scream, they didn't bother to put their boots on. Two men had the nail stuck completely thru the foot while another who had fallen to the ground ended up sitting on a nail with more swearing and yelling. When the nails were pulled out, being jagged, it caused such pain that two men passed out.

Rocky witnessed the mayhem and heard Haltomier say, "that does it, somebody has it out for us. Not only does the sniper kill two of us, but he also wants to torture us. Come daylight, we're going to scout the area and kill this bastard."

Rocky returned to the squad's hideout and revealed the result of the traps. When it became clear that the outlaws were coming to hunt them down at dawn. The squad picked up and rode away for the day. Willie was the only one who stayed behind. When the outlaws left camp to hunt for the sniper, he doubled back to their camp. After climbing another pine tree overlooking the camp, he attached a bundle with a red bandana to the tree and cut some branches so the red bandana could be seen from the squad's hideout some 150 yards away.

By supper time, the outlaws returned to camp. Haltomier and Bendix were not happy, and both were talking of getting their individual gangs to light out. It was Dooling who convinced them to wait till morning before running away from a well-planned heist.

The squad was watching the outlaws and when their supper was just about ready, Jake said, "Furman take your long-range rifle and spot that red bandana on the pine tree overlooking the campfire." "Yeah, I got it in my scope set to 150 yards."

"Good, shoot it and don't miss. You boys cover your ears and get behind a tree for protection." Furman smiled, took careful aim and pulled the trigger. The shot rang out and almost simultaneously the earth shook ------KAABOOM/BOOM/BOOM. Every outlaw was thrown to the ground. The campfire was blown out, the cooking stew and beans were blown off, and the horses pulled off their tethers and disappeared at a full gallop. The outlaws were either groaning or vomiting or were silent from losing consciousness. Several tried to get up but were so dizzy that they sat back down. Then Haltomier saw Bendix. The pine treetop had been blown off the main part of the tree and was implanted in Bendix's lower belly. Bendix's mouth was open, his face in total horror, as he had both hands on the tree's stem.

Jake assessed the devastation, "huum, very effective. Guess on day two, everyone can say it was a bad hair day, heh?" Furman answered, "three down and several disabled."

That night, after the outlaws had went to their bedrolls, the squad went to work. Jake was watching the camp in case an outlaw caught his men working about. Rocky walked over to the saddles, cut off all the cinch buckles, and brought them back to the squad's hideout. Willie and Furman had cut open the back wall of the food tent and poured kerosene all over the opened bags of food. Walt had gotten access to the case of whiskey and had opened all twelve bottles and poured each one on the ground.

In the morning of day three, when opening the food tent to get the coffee, Haltomier yelled, "what the hell, the food is ruined, the whiskey is gone, and this tent was entered. Who was on guard watch last night? Dooling answered, "it was one of my men" as he pointed to the one called Mortimer. "Sorry boss, I must have dozed off a bit." Haltomier was furious, drew his pistol, and nonchalantly shot Mortimer in the heart. That does it, boys, we're all out of here. We'll move closer to town and attack the banks tomorrow, a day early. Some of you go find our horses and the rest of you pack up camp."

When the horses were all found and brought back to camp, some of the men started to saddle them. "Hey, the cinch buckles are all gone, we can't hook up the cinches." Haltomier added, "then we ride bareback but we get out." Dooling adds, "the men are all dizzy and can't ride bareback, they'll fall off their horses and break their necks. I'm not dizzy and can ride bareback, I'll go to town and get vittles, whiskey, cinch buckles, leather straps, leather punches and rivets. I'll be back in three hours. We'll repair the cinches, be able to ride out for the attack, and escape after we get the payroll money."

The squad saw Dooling take off and mounted up to catch him before he got through the squad's ranks. After being captured, Jake told him to scream like he was being tortured. "Like hell I am!" "Suit yourself, Rocky come here with your knife, cut one of his nipples off and peel a two-inch strip of skin off." "Yeah sure, lawmen don't do those things." Rocky stepped up, tore his shirt open, without time for Dooling to reflect, the nipple came off and a strip of skin was being cut. Dooling let off the scream that even surprised the squad members. Jake added, "make it louder Dooling, I want your buddies to hear the fear in your voice. As Rocky extended the peeled strip to his belly, the screeching, yelling and begging got unbearably loud. "That's enough Rocky, I'm sure the gang heard enough. Now go looking for a hornet's nest or a rattle snake or both—no skunks for crying out loud."

By the end of day 3, Furman says "2 shot by Jake, Bendix caught a treetop, Mortimer shot by Haltomier, one captured and many disabled and demoralized."

During the night Walt and Willie set up trip wires which were anchored to the double triggers of sawed-off shotguns. One setup was on the trail to the horses and the second trip wire setup was on the path to the bushes. There were two well beaten paths for quick escape out of the camp. Around 4AM Furman and Rocky were both each carrying a burlap bag. One was buzzing and the other was rattling. Arriving next to the sleeping outlaws, Rocky throws the open bag, carrying the rattler, at one of the outlaws, as Furman smashes his bag against a tree and heaves it, with the bag open, into the outlaws' camp.

The resultant response was a masterpiece. The rattler managed to bite three outlaws before one finally shot it. The hornets were everywhere and stinging with a vengeance. The outlaws knew they had to escape. They couldn't go behind the camp because of a mountain of boulders, could not go forward into the hands of the torturers, so they were all running sideways to the bushes and towards the horses. Suddenly, bang/bang and bang/bang. There was no screaming or swearing and Furman says, "gosh, two more down, that makes six dead, one captured and ten to go, but many not worth a damn in a fight."

So, Jake finally said, "this is day four and the day of reckoning. I'm going to give them a final chance to surrender after this last terrorizing attack. Rocky, attach these three sticks of dynamite individually to arrows. Sneak up to 50 yards and lob an arrow with the fuse lit into their camp. Herb will be with you to light the fuse and defend you in case they attack you. Put cotton in your ears and hide behind a boulder for protection against a concussion. When you're done, stay put and the remainder of the squad will join you at 50 yards."

Herb and Rocky with each holding a lit cheroot in their mouths as lighting fodder. Once in place, Rocky let go an arrow and placed it in the roof of a tent. The explosion knocked every standing outlaw to the ground. The second loaded arrow was randomly sent into the camp but somehow found its unintended target, Haltomier's belt buckle, and when the dynamite went off the leader's mid-section was atomized into gore and soup. Whereas his genitals and legs went one way, and his shoulders, arms and head went another way. Jake was looking at the result and was about to call Rocky off when the third and last arrow took off. This time the loaded arrow landed in the campfire and the outlaws were again thrown to the ground, deaf, dizzy and their clothes on fire. The camp was totally devastated and razed. The tents were all torn up and their contents were spread all over the area. By viewing all this, Jake said, "hey, you pricks of misery, are you done in. Either you surrender now or I'm not responsible for obliterating the rest of you!"

Some angry spokesman yelled, "come and get us, we'll take most of you out before we go down—come on, show us how big you are, face to face. No more long-range sniping, bear traps, nails, dynamite, cut cinches, hornets, ruined food and whiskey, rattle snakes, trip wires and flying dynamite. Now it's time for face to face guns."

Jake yells his response, "suit yourself, but remember we don't put our lives in danger to save the lives of killer outlaws. We're coming."

Jake tells his squad and Herb to load two OO Buckshot in the pump magazine, followed by two #4 Buck next in the magazine and one #4 Buck in the chamber. "We're all going to sneak to 40 yards and each of us will shoot three times, throwing each three #4 Buckshot at the camp-that's 27 pellets per shell, or 81 pellets per man or a total of 486 pellets. This won't kill them but will stun and mangle them. After our three shots, we rush the camp and point our shotguns with two OO Buckshot ready to put any man down who goes for his pistol or rifle. I predict that they won't be in any condition to fight. Any questions?"

No one spoke and after their shotguns were loaded to specs, each answered in turn, "ready boss."

The squad followed Jakes plan and by the time they rushed the camp, the outlaws were all in a state of shock. Several had lost eyes and ears and their clothing was all ripped apart. The bodies were peppered with pellets imbedded deep in the skin and would require painful probing to remove them, if the doc, had the patience. The outlaws were all manacled and moved fifty yards away and a new camp was established. They started a fire, brought all the horses together, prepared dinner, and several men were repairing the cut cinches with straps, punches and rivets. The saddlebags and the outlaws' pockets were searched and an amazing sum of $1500 was found which was divided amongst the five Marshals and the sheriff. Guns were gathered, bodies and body parts were wrapped in tent canvas, and loaded onto their one utility wagon.

After a nice dinner of ham, fried potatoes, beans, coffee and canned peaches; Jake took the opportunity to have a special meeting. "Well boys, we managed to capture 17 outlaws, dead or alive, and Herb suspects that each outlaw will likely have a $500 reward and the leaders at $1,000 each. If that's the case, then we're likely to collect $10,000—divided six ways comes to +-$1,650 each. Remember, the guns and horses go to Captain Ennis, to pay for your salaries and benefits. Now the second item is this. This is my last caper as a US Marshal. I'm retiring."

There was dead silence in the camp, and

it was Willie who spoke, "we're sad to see you go, but we understand, and each of us knew this day would come. You've got a lovely wife, family and a heck of a business to take care of. But we'll still miss you."

"Thanks boys, now I have recommended that Furman take control of the squad. Rocky will still be available when his talents are needed, and he will be paid by the day on the job, and by his share of the rewards like each of you. Now, let's close up camp and deliver these bums to the Federal jail for disposition to their wanted communities, where they will be prosecuted for existing crimes. Judge Hobart won't have jurisdiction since their crimes were committed out of his district. Gathering and planning a heist will not hold mustard to prosecute them in town. Lastly, Sheriff Bixby will process the reward vouchers."

Furman adds, "that's it boys, let's get going and we'll be home for supper. Besides, I think a massive hay harvest is waiting Jake, heh."

***

CHAPTER 10

THE RANCH

Jake arrived home by supper time. Hannah was jumping with joy and was planting one hot kiss after another. When he finally took in a full breath, he said, "why are you so passionate, I've only been gone a week?" Hannah just started crying, "it's just the superstitious idea that when it's a final caper, the odds are against you to survive. I'm sorry to be so emotional, it's probably the hormones of pregnancy talking."

"I don't care what the reason is. I'm glad to be here with you because I missed you as well. Now, let's have some supper, I'm starved." "Ok, I have a nice meal ready, I went to the butcher today after my writing class and bought some fresh T-bone steaks, and we'll have that with some fresh onion soup, baked potatoes, boiled beets, with a dessert of tapioca pudding and coffee. After supper, you're going to tell me the details of your jungle warfare and then I'll bring you up to date on the harvest."

After a fine meal, Jake went thru the four-day siege they forced the outlaws to endure. From the first shooting surprise to the last shotgun volleys, Jake described the different terrorizing events. Hannah was attentive to every detail and was enthusiastically taking notes. She only interrupted him twice, when the dynamite was used. "Where did you get dynamite?" "Greg had six sticks left over after they capped the well and I thought they might be useful as a jungle warfare ultimate tool. Let me tell you, they were very disruptive and demoralizing, when the outlaws saw the treetop impaled in Bendix's belly or Haltomier cut in half."

Once Jake was done, Hannah said, "This will cover the last chapter of my book. Then I'll add an epilogue and will send it to Isabella.

Apparently, Osmer and Peabody are setting the book to type and will be ready for my last two shipments to publish 500 paperbacks."

"Wow, there's no turning back now, your book will be published."

"Yes, and Isabella tells me that the story will sell like hot-cakes. Now, let me bring you up to date with haying season. The cropboys had been mowing all day and are planning to continue mowing each day till the entire 1st crop of 600 acres of prime hay is down. The drought was now helping the harvest. The hay is mature, the land is dry, and the hay will dry in 24-36 hours from the hot sun, dry parched air and light breeze over the south Texas plains."

"When I rode in, I could have sworn I saw five balers, I thought we had four."

"Well that is a long story. Mister Heinz saw an ad in a Rio Grande Valley newspaper. It appeared that a small crop farmer was retiring, and he put his equipment, baler, hay loader, side rake and hay wagon for sale. Heinz bought it and sent word, thru Donna coming home, that the four pieces had arrived and would sell them for $425. Clayton never hesitated, he opened the safe, took out the cash, and went straight to the feed store. Bromley Freighting followed him home with the four pieces."

"Fantastic, so, are we ready to start baling?"

"Yes, the tedders worked all afternoon, and with no morning dew, the side rakes will start making rows by 7AM. We'll have hay on the baling platforms by 9AM at the latest."

"How is the staffing set up to cover all the positions?"

"Here is the list prepared by Clayton. It's broken down in three sections"

1. Harvesting. 2 cutters, 2 tedders/finish rake, 2 on side rakes, 6 to load hay and stack it on wagons, 1 to transfer wagons from field to baling platform, and 1 to unload wagons.
2. Baling. 2 men to control horses powering the cam(Rocky and Red Flower), 4 men on each baler(5 balers = 20 men), and 3 men to load boxcars via conveyor once local ranchers are loaded for the day.

3. Accessory personnel. You and Clayton as floaters. Unassigned men to include the blacksmith Washington and Yvonne. Four pregnant gals. Erna and Laura to bring water to field horses and workers. Natalie Coombs to bring mid-morning and mid-afternoon snacks to all workers. The mechanic to support the implements, oil, grease and repairs.

'Whoa, I have three questions; what are you doing, why only one man to unload wagons and why are four pregnant gals working on the balers?"

"My job will be to take the cash and keep the sales documented as far as which rancher received how much hay, for future reference. Clayton expects every rancher, for 10 miles east and west of town, to be arriving with hay wagons and cash. Each wagon load is paid cash—50 cents a bale. I'm also responsible to keep fresh water at the baling sites. I'll also be doing prep work for the cook, such as peeling potatoes and cutting up vegetables when I have free time. I will also be 'wanna the gopher.' You know, wanna go for this, for that, and get this man."

Now, as for the four pregnant gals, Camilla, Josie, Donna and Sandra. They insist on working their shifts like everyone." "But they're pregnant, and when did Donna and Sandra get pregnant?"

"Pregnancy is not a disabling disease, it's a temporary condition, and I'm sure that Donna and Sandra didn't get pregnant last night, heh!"

"Now to explain why we need only one man to unload hay wagons. Stanley designed a three-prong adjustable hook that can be imbedded in the hay and then one horse drags the twitch off the wagon onto the concrete floor next to the balers via an overhead gantry. It will take two twitches to empty 90% of the load in short order."

"Sounds like this operation will take close to 50 men and cost $150 a day in labor. Do we have any spare workers if we need more help?"

"Yes, your squad said they'll be glad to help if we need them. That also includes Clifton

Gibson and Greg Webb. Plus, don't forget that all the workers are eager to work overtime over their 8-hour days."

"Has Clayton computed how long this first crop will take?"

"Of course, he says, assuming we end up with 300 extra tons on the first crop, the 900 tons will take 20 days as long as each baler can put out 15 bales per hour."

"This may be ridiculous, but how did he come down to 20 days?"

"The math goes: Each baler = 15 bales/hour or 120 bales/8-hour shift. 120 bales equal 3 tons per baler. There being five balers we should produce 15 tons per 8-hour shift or 45 tons per 24-hour period. Now, in my book 45 tons times 20 days comes to 900 tons of hay in 20 days, heh? And if we can't put out 15 bales per hour per baler, it's going to take us more than 20 days."

"Sounds like this is a given that the labor will cost $3,000 for 20 harvesting days. Even if we harvest the expected 600 tons on the first crop, at $20 a ton that comes to $12,000. If the first crop yield is higher than expected, as Clayton thinks, the increase in labor will be offset by the larger crop for sale. I still think we need more backup workers!"

"OOPS, I forgot, Kevin Wood will be here early tomorrow to start picking up hay. He pointed out that this is the slow season for cattle ranchers, and he has a dozen men loafing around. If we need their help, he can spare six cowhands a day that would be happy to earn a few extra dollars. This order came from Galvin himself. By the way!"

"Wow, sounds like Galvin meant it when he said he would make things right. Let's get some sleep. It's going to be a hectic first day." "What no loving." "Well if you insist, but only once. We need to conserve our energy." "Yeah, right?"

***

By 6AM, Rocky and Red Flower were harnessing horses. The cook had been serving coffee, eggs, and bacon since 5:30. The two side rakes were first off to prepare the rows. The loaders were hitched to the wagons and were off to pick up their first load. The first load of hay arrived at 8:30AM and Clayton showed how the unloading hook saved a lot of labor. Each man's position was explained by Clayton as the other teams were watching and waiting for their first load.

Jake was assigned to learn how to pass the strings and return them to his partner on the other side of the bale. Then he learned how to make a durable slipknot that will hold when a man picks up the 50-pound bale by the strings. Jake eventually became the float for the five balers. When the two men or women were getting behind, he would pitch in to help. Anytime a worker needed a privy break, he would take over the worker's job. When the pregnant gals were slowing down, he would send them on a water break and take over their job.

The ranchers' wagons were arriving in droves. Clayton would line them up, so each baler had its own line based on the last to arrive being sent to the end of the shortest line. To keep it honest, once a wagon was in line, it stayed in that line till they got to the baler and started loading their wagons. For the most part, most wagons arrived with two men and could load and stack their own wagon. When a wagon arrived with only one rider, Jake or Clayton would help out to keep the system going.

The bale count was the responsibility of the arriving cowhand. Depending on the wagon size, the total count varied and the price of 50 cents a bale was based on each wagon's count. Fortunately, the ranchers had modified the basic ranch wagon to hold more hay, and most could hold a ton, or 40 bales.

The ranchers had gotten the message that cash payment was expected before departure. This was never a problem, and Hannah would give the cowboys a receipt for every load. Jake and Clayton were surprised that ranchers were coming from farther than anticipated. The lines lasted till nightfall for the first five days. During the night shift, workers were transferring bales to the nearest boxcar for sale to Dallas, or filling the sheds. At daybreak, when the local ranchers arrived, they resumed loading their wagons.

Clayton had planned to fill the sheds with all three crops, but had not explained this yet to Jake.

Finally, Clayton said, "With both sheds full, we have the choice to choose the feed for our cattle/horses, or sell it to our neighbors or to our customers in Dallas. Forage nutrition is highest with second crop hay, 1st crop hay is in-between and straw is lowest." He made it clear, that our herd was priority with high nutrition hay, the local ranchers came in second with 1st crop hay, and the Dallas customers got the leftovers with contracts only at the end of the harvest season.

"As far as straw, in the winter some horses are less active and get overweight with hay. Straw is the best way to limit their calories. Plus, some horses have to be munching on some feed longer than others and hay is not the feed to use in these heavy eaters. Also, when we have a sick calf, it is nice to make a bed of straw, to keep them off the cold ground in the nursery lean-to."

Hannah was busy running in the office to cash out ranchers, and keeping the water bucket full of cold well water. When she had a minute, she could be seen sitting on the porch peeling potatoes, shucking corn, slicing carrots and other vegetables. The cook's helper was delivering and picking up finished pots on a regular basis. Jake insisted, that after the last wagon left at night, she was directed to her bed. Jake managed to put twelve continuous hours each day.

The night shift was monitored by Clayton's crop foreman and seemed to function well under the lamps. The field workers would work till midnight and would quit when the hay supply next to the balers would last till daybreak. The early field worker's shift would often start at predawn and would last ten hours, that way the second shift would finish around midnight. Once the harvest started, every worker was paid time and a half after eight hours on the job. Keeping track of overtime pay was another duty added to Hannah's shoulders.

Each hay plot covered 100 acres. As soon as a plot was harvested, Irving Gallaway and his workers would open the dam of one holding pond and flood the plot. The first flooding was three inches well contained by berms. Afterwards, he would flood the plot with one and a half inches every five days. The results were dramatic, regrowth was quick to appear and, despite the drought, was showing signs of a good second harvest. The streams were still replenishing the holding ponds and the cattle water troughs were holding full. The cost to the county was insignificant compared to the value it was producing. Thanks to the county agent and his workers, they were able to commandeer the flooding program till Clayton could take it over after the first crop was in.

Ten days into the harvest, the likely half-way point, the men were getting tired of the long hours. Jake never hesitated, he hired Stanley and Yvonne Washington, the full squad and the six cowhands from the Galvin ranch. Natalie Coombs worked the same shift as Walt and Clifton Gibson was working a full eight-hour shift. Donna alternating with Josie were added to the office to help Hannah out.

Knowing that the squad could be called

on assignment anytime, Jake passed the word around that he would pay $3 for an 8-hour day with meals and $4 for four hours of cumulative overtime. Neighboring homesteaders with farming experience were showing up and the regular workers got relief. The pace never faltered, and the worker's morale was solid for the remainder of the harvest.

After twenty days of continuous work, the first crop was done. The total tonnage came to an amazing 900 tons of dry hay. The ranchers managed to take 500 tons because no one believed that there would be a second crop due to the drought. Jake kept 100 tons of first crop hay and 300 tons were shipped to several of the Dallas distributors who were desperate to fill contracts and even paid a premium of $25 a ton instead of the going rate of $20 a ton. The reason for not keeping of the first crop were finally explained by Clayton. "Jake, the first crop is 70% stems and 30% leaves and seeds. The second crop will be the opposite with 30% stems and 70% leaves and seeds which have the higher nutritional value than stems. So, we shipped the lower nutritional hay and we'll keep the higher quality for us and our local ranchers who will be back once they know the advantage of second crop hay. Alfalfa was more evenly distributed between stems and leaves/stems."

Alfalfa was a higher nutritious forage that sold for $25 a ton locally and $30 a ton to distributors. Alfalfa dried well with the drought and this became important knowledge for all to learn. Baling alfalfa that was not completely dry could lead to mold and mildew. When this happened, cattle and horses could become severely ill with gaseous distention and some could even die. Fortunately, careful inspection before its sale guaranteed dry forage that did not ferment to mold.

The workers all benefited from overtime and every man signed up for the second crop and even the oats harvest. Clayton laid off as many idle hands till the next crop. He kept a full staff of cow punchers and crop farmers as they were all year-round workers.

***

Waiting for August 1st, when the hay would be ready, the cropboys planted the 100 acres of oats. Afterwards, they started cultivating a new 100-acre plot for future expansion. The other milestone was the completion of the entire ranch's barbwire fencing.

During the six-week waiting period, the cowhands were busy keeping the herd on residual grasses where water was accessible. Also breeding season started. The purebred Hereford, Durham and Black Angus were segregated into different paddocks. After two estrus cycles, the purebred herds were released to mix with the entire herd.

When the preparations began for the second crop, the crop men had finished cultivating the seventh 100-acre plot of hay. The alfalfa trial during the first crop was very popular with the ranchers who wanted the extra nutrition during winter months, and this new plot would be reserved for alfalfa.

So, what did the Duo do during their six-week waiting period? Well Hannah finished her book and shipped the last chapter and epilogue to Isabella. Now time would tell how effective the marketing plan would be in selling the book. Isabella was certain that it would take off like hot cakes and even authorized the second printing ahead of proven sales. Now with the second crop around the corner, Hannah took the time off to rest. Her pregnancy, now four months along, was progressing without complications.

Jake spent much time with Greg. He needed to learn the market and negotiating methods with refineries. He took two trips, to Houston and Dallas, with Greg. They were able to get signed contracts with two new private refineries at 85 cents a barrel. Each contract was for ten thousand barrels, which was all new business and would wait a bit since Greg was still filling old contracts with four other refineries. On their way home, Greg had mentioned his fears that the crude oil prices were about to crash. "You see Jake, the big oil companies are activating their dormant refineries. Once these refineries start flooding the market with their products, the price of crude could go as low as 50 cents a barrel."

"Well if that happens, fill our storage shed and then close down the wells after the contracts are filled. During the negotiations, I could not understand why you insisted on money up front. Now I know, we have $17,000 in the bank and if the prices drop, we're protected." "Yes, and that's the same reason why all my old contracts are paid up front."

***

The preparations for the second crop started. The mechanic and blacksmith had spent the last six weeks repairing and maintaining the implements. Rocky had taken one of the cowboys, by the name of Buster, on as a wrangler apprentice because he had hidden 'whispering' talents, and was able to speak to horses. Together with Red Flower they had repaired all the damaged harnesses.

The workers started arriving a week ahead of time. The food was good, friendships were resumed, and many of the men were lucky to get odd jobs at full pay. The evening before the start day, Jake showed up at the cookshack during supper. He commandeered the room with a short speech. He basically thanked the workers for returning and gave them all a bonus for signing up. Every worker in the room received two twenty-dollar double Eagles. Clayton later said, "Jake, that's a fine touch that guarantees your workers will always have your best interest at heart and will give that extra effort without being asked."

The second crop's harvest started with alfalfa that was stored in one of the sheds. The ranchers took some more on a trial basis but were waiting for the hay's second crop. The ranchers were arriving early in the mornings and were all loaded by noon. Then the conveyor was started, and the sheds were filling with top quality hay. The ranchers finally realized that this second crop, like alfalfa, had higher nutritional values, and as the word got around, ranchers kept coming throughout the entire second harvest.

The harvest was much smoother now that every worker was accustomed with his or her jobs. Clayton finally devised a useful manner of scheduling workers. He had two divisions. Regular workers who would put eight hours a day and the other included those who wished to do overtime. He had three charts for each day and usually had two days-work scheduled ahead of time. Hannah would check each 8-hour shift and record the workers time at the end of their shift.

Hannah explained to Jake how the most popular and busy shift was the 7AM to 3PM day shift. Overtime on that shift occurred when ranchers were done loading for the day, and the overtime workers had to come in to start the conveyor to transfer the bales to the sheds. These overtime workers came from the next shift, or had been called into work early. The second shift, 3PM to 11PM was the evening shift manned by all regular workers including the three workers handling the conveyor and stacking the hay in the shed. It was rare for overtimers to be on this shift. Now the night shift, 11PM to 7AM, was mostly manned by overtime workers except for two workers and the night shift foreman.

The field workers did not pick up hay between 11PM and 7AM, but throughout the other two shifts, and excess of hay was delivered to the baling platform. This was the supply of hay being processes by the night shift. It was well planned, for the night shift never ran out of hay and the balers never had down time.

The second crop took 17 days and yielded 750 tons of excellent quality hay. The ranchers had purchased 250 tons of hay and 50 tons of alfalfa. The remainder went into the sheds. Unbeknownst to Jake, Clayton had convinced the county agent to flood the second crop's first 100 acres harvested. It was an experiment to see if regrowth would occur before the winter dormant months. The flooding continued every five days as had been done for the second crop and the oats acreage.

After the second crop was completed, within two weeks the slower process of harvesting 100 acres of oats started. The processes that took extra time was the mowing/bundling, followed by threshing and winnowing. On top of that, once the oats were in the bags, the straw had to be collected and then baled just like the hay was. The bottom line was that this was a summer crop, harvested in the fall after the hay/alfalfa crops, and yielding the precious horse grain—oats.

The oats crop yielded 100 tons of straw and thirty-five 25-pound bags of oats. The oats would now be saved for ranch use to feed the large remuda of cowpunching, riding, and work horses. The straw was housed in one of the sheds and would come in handy with the winter drought. It became a supplement in cattle to make the hay last longer and also feed inactive horses.

The drought had delayed winter and the 100-acre experiment of producing a third crop was a surprise. Clayton finally showed the acreage to the Duo. "This grass is now 16-18 inches high and we're going start mowing it tomorrow. Now, had we started the first crop sooner than June 1st, we could have had a mature third crop. Actually, looking back, our first crop was way too mature and had too much stem low in nutrition. Next season we'll start the first crop by May 10th, and we'll end up with three good crops as long as we add a quick and light layer of phosphate between each crop. There is money to be made with this land if we use our heads."

"Excellent idea, now what happens to this 800+ acres during the winter?"

"We continue cultivating new land and we spread horse manure over the entire crop acreage we plan to harvest next season."

"Where are we going to get horse manure, we've picked up everything within, three miles of the ranch?"

"Ah hah, that's why you pay me big bucks!"

"I have found two new sources. In town, every store and building has a barn or day-shed behind their place of business. Did you ever notice the pile of manure next to all these small structures? Well, we are purchasing them at 50 cents a load—that's the extra-large transferring manure spreader load! I've also purchased a huge 100-year old composted pile that I bartered hay for." "Where and who?" "Galvin's Circle G Ranch." "Well, I'll be damned." "Yeah, Kevin Wood made the offer during the first harvest.

He was extremely generous, and we did very well to take his offer. The boys are getting a third extra-large transferring manure spreader next week. That way we'll use one in town and two hauling to Galvin's ranch. I'll put two men on the one in town. We'll have one man transferring and spreading the long-haul loads while two men load the other manure spreader."

"Is it a problem finding men for this job."

"Heck no, the original threesome, Daryl, Merle and Enis always have first dibs. Now with this being winter employment, I have eight other laid-off workers who have applied for the job. Since they all need the work, I've given each of them some days every week. All in all, you can count on the 800 acres to be fully fertilized by spring."

After a short three days, the third crop was processed, and some 40 tons were baled and stored in the sheds. October would highlight the crossbreeding show that Jake had planned for the Circle H Ranch.

***

During the second crop harvest, Hannah

had passed out a flyer announcing the crossbreeding show at the ranch on October 15. The flyer mentioned a discussion on the beneficial advantages of crossbreeding Texas Longhorns, a full lunch surprise and options to join a new cattlemen's association. For 'show day' preparation, Jake arranged for a tent/canopy to be assembled in the front yard, to ward off the hot sun; and the construction of four viewing corrals to hold: three purebred animals and the fourth to hold Texas Longhorns steers mixed with crossbreed steers. The morning of the event saw ranchers arriving with their wives, foreman, and selected cowhands. At registration 21 ranchers registered with their guests. After registration, Hannah told the cook to be ready to feed 90 people at noon.

Jake rang the bell at 10AM and started the meeting. "Welcome, and thanks for coming today. By the end of the day, I hope to convince you to make a drastic change to your cattle herd. I know this will be an uphill battle since you and your ancestors have been raising Texas Longhorns for hundreds of years. But change is part of life and if you want to survive as cattle ranchers, you will have to change with the times."

"To start, what is a crossbreed? It is the mix of a purebred beef bull, such as a Hereford or Durham Short Horn, with a Texas Longhorn cow or heifer. The result is an animal that shares the best genetic inheritance of both breeds. So, we know what we are talking about, look behind me as the cowboys walk three animals—a Texas Longhorn mature cow, a two-year-old Hereford bull and a two-year-old Durham Short Horn bull." Hannah noted the eyeballs staring at the two purebred bulls.

"So, let's talk about purebred and crossbreed bulls.

- These bulls are much more docile than Longhorn bulls with their massive and dangerous horns.
- They are aggressive breeders.
- They pass on a 'polled' gene which shortens the Longhorns by 50% each generation.

- They sell for $60 a head for breeding purposes."

"Now, let's talk about cows and heifers.

- The Longhorn cows and crossbreed heifers have a much easier time calving a crossbred calf.
- All cows and heifers have a higher insemination rate.
- Crossbreed heifers will have a regular recurring estrus every month till bred.
- Shortened horns will make the herd safer to work."

"And finally, let's talk about the crossbreed calf.

- The newborn calves are active within an hour, more energetic and alert than native calves, and more aggressive in the early weeks of suckling. They start eating grass within three weeks of birth which is a full month ahead of native calves.

- Being that they share the genes of two breeds, they are more resistant to disease, especially Texas Longhorn fever.
- They can get more nutrition out of the Texas local grasses than native calves.
- They grow faster on our southern ranges. This yields a higher animal total weight at any age—which means more money for you.
- The Durham is the highest milk producer. For a cow who loses their calf, this breed makes an excellent docile 'milch' cow."

"So, you say, why bother? Well the obvious answer is that it means more money for you. You will sell an animal with 20% more meat on its bones. Plus, the meat will have greater value per pound. Let's talk about the different grades of beef as we approach the mid 1890's.

NATIVE: The Texas Longhorn is an old generation of unimproved beef. It is stringy, extra lean, low on flavor and basically tough to chew. It is eatable especially if you don't know any better. But, people today know better. After lunch today, you will all know better."

SELECT: This is produced by crossing a purebred Hereford or Durham bull with a Texas Longhorn—or first-generation crossbreed. It is not as lean since it has marbling which is fat between the meat fibers. This marbling is classic of crossbreeds and purebreds. It imparts flavor to the meat as well as tenderness."

CHOICE: A second generation crossbreed changes the consistency of the meat even more. There is more marbling, more tenderness and more flavor. If you castrate a crossbred 2nd generation bull, at two years of age, you'll be selling this animal as choice grade beef."

PRIME: This grade of beef is the ultimate goal. It is a third generation or higher of crossbreeding. These animals are approaching the beef quality of purebred Herefords and Durhams. The meat has plenty of marbling and the flavor/tenderness is none to be matched. The customers in the East want this meat. The highest demand is the Prime Chateaubriand. This is the cut of meat from the thickest end of the backstrap tenderloin—or filet mignon as it is also known."

"The next part of this meeting is the show and tell portion. Let's move to the corrals to see these animals. Notice in the first two corrals the purebred Hereford and Durham Short Horn bulls and heifers. These are 18 month and 2-year old animals. Notice their shape, square bulky backs, massive hind quarters, forequarters heavy on the shoulders and short stalky legs. The Herefords are polled whereas the Short Horns have +- 6-8 inch straight horns. The Hereford hide is a mix of burgundy or bright red and white, and the Short Horn hide is a uniform light to dark brown."

"The third corral is the purpose of this meeting. Here you have the 1st generation crossbreed steers. Look at the difference between these six- month old crossbreed and the six-month old Texas Longhorn steers. Some are clearly the product of breeding with Herefords whereas some are a mix with Short Horns." Hannah whispers to Jake, "these ranchers are not just looking, they are mussitating amongst themselves." "Dear, this is not time for a vocabulary lesson, what in hell is mussitating?" "Oh sorry, I meant mumbling amongst themselves."

"Moving on, this fourth corral holds my newest addition from Mr. Powell. These are beef cattle from Scotland called Black Angus. They have the same body shape and size as the Hereford and Durham's, but the hide is black. This breed adds a third genetic inheritance to the crossbreeding process. It also adds a new cattle quality, these animals have the ability to hold water longer and go between more distant watering locations. The addition of black color in the herd will add a unique identifying characteristic to my crossbreed herd."

Having just been given a signal from the cook, Jake announced that lunch was ready, "now, you will have a real treat. Yes, we are serving Prime beef. This is a three-year old steer crossbreed beef sent to us by Emmitt Powel for this event (more on this man later). Every rancher will have a piece of Chateaubriand filet mignon. Your guests will have a piece of the regular filet mignon. You will also have as much fresh 'beef round' sliced to your taste. The center of the round will be rare, and the outside will be medium. Choose the thickness you wish as the cook's assistant will slice it for you. Side dishes will include mashed or baked potato, sliced carrots with fresh buttered rolls and coffee. There is plenty of food and please be sure that you have tasted all the beef we are presenting."

Tables had been set under the sun canopy during the show and tell portion at the corrals. After all the 70 guests and all the 20 ranch employees were served, the Duo sat there and watched their guests. No one was speaking, then the moans and groans started. Eventually the exclamations started—Jeeese, this is incredible, tasty, tender, I've never had anything like this, dear we need to grow these animals, amazing, what a great idea, I'm making contact with this Emmitt Powel today."

With a cake dessert and coffee, Jake resumed the meeting. "Let's now have a question and answer period and I will then finish the day with a final surprise."

Q. "Who is this man Emmitt Powell, where does he live and how much does he charge for these purebred and crossbreed bulls and heifers?"

A. "Well Kevin, that's a mouthful of a first question. Emmitt Powell is an innovative rancher who lives close by just west of San Antonio. Years ago, he started crossbreeding his Texas Longhorns with Hereford and Durham bulls. Now five years later, he is finally selling purebred and crossbreed building stock. I got all my animals from him last year as I just received forty Black Angus bulls and heifers. He charges $60 for purebred Hereford or Durham bulls, $40 for their heifers. For crossbreed bulls the price is $50 and the heifers for $40. The Black Angus will be available next year at the same prices."

Q. "With the drought, some of us are not sure we can feed the extra heads with the hay we have?"

A. "Not a problem, I have plenty of extra hay. If necessary, I'll give it to you. Don't let this drought hold you back."

Q. "Do you have any for sale?"

A. "No, not yet. If you want a guarantee, I will sell you breeding stock next spring, and at a discount, because we are neighbors and the animals will only be one-year-old's."

Q. "Regarding the drought, will you sell us some water?"

A. "No. I don't sell water; I'll give it to you. I don't own the water; I use it and I'm willing to give you what I can spare. Get yourselves some transfer tanks and you can load them off my holding ponds."

Q. "Are the beef buyers in pace with this change?"

A. "Yes, I've talked to several and they are all eager to get this new beef and are willing to compensate you accordingly for quality beef."

Q. "If we join in, are we being pioneers of a new breed?"

A. "In our area we would be pioneers. Crossbreeding is starting all over Texas. Mr. Powell is trying to start an area between San Antonio and New Braunsfel as the center for crossbred beef. If this happens, we'll start our own Cattlemen's Association which will have the control to set prices that the buyers will have to accept."

Q. "This is so new; can you go over the time frame to develop a new herd?"

A. "Sure. You'll take the first two years to raise as many bulls as you can. The third year you have to choose if you want to raise steers or whether you want to sell bulls. You may not be the only rancher with the same plan, but you'll get top dollar for two and three-year-old steers.

So, you can sell bulls within eighteen months, like I will do prematurely next spring, or sell steers within two or three years."

Q. Assuming I'm lucky and can get a starting herd from Mr. Powell, what is the first thing I need to do?"

A. "Get rid of your Texas Longhorn bulls, now. Before the drought affects the price of beef, bring those bulls to market. You don't need to winter those full-size bulls with hay you purchased. The amount you get will help defray the cost of the purebred and crossbreed animals. Also, build some separate paddocks for breeding your purebred heifers with their own bulls before releasing them to mix with the herd."

Q. "Our Texas Longhorn bulls are historically able to breed 10 cows per bull. What is the ratio with purebred Hereford, Durham, and crossbreed bulls?"

A. "One bull per twenty cows/heifers. Within two estrus cycles, you'll have over 95% insemination or better."

Q. "I did not see any evidence of burning ear buds, but your entire herd has been ear tagged. Can you explain?"

A. "We decided that burning ear buds was creating an artificial appearance for our new herd. We want people to see the new horn length and appearance. This is the natural crossbreed look. As far as ear tagging, if you convert your herd to crossbreeds, you really need to ID every animal. At the first roundup, brand your calves for possession and ear tag the calf and mother for ID. We even ear tagged all our bulls.

The reason is so you can identify the generation of each crossbred animal and keep a record of this information. For day to day use, any animal's good or bad characteristics can be identified with the ear tag. We use this for culling the herd. We make a list of the numbers that go on the culling list, and when the time comes, the cowboys cut these animals out of the herd. Ear tags take the guessing out of the picture. Raising cattle is now the business of raising the best animals, and ear tags allow you to do this."

Q. "So, what should we call this new breed?"

A. "As it is called in other parts of this state, 'Texas Crossbreeds.'"

Q. "I don't have a question; I have a statement to make. As many of you know, my boss is in prison till next spring. I communicate with him by letter each month. When I told him of this upcoming meeting and how he would want me to deal with this idea, he sent me his answer. He said he had gone to the prison library and read several books on the subject. He told me not to hesitate, to buy what was needed and to start converting his herd. He said, this was the only way of the future if cattle ranchers were to survive in the 1900's. So, I'll be the first to send a telegram to Mr. Powell and order a complement of bulls to cover my herd of 400 breed-able cows and heifers. I also firmly believe that starting our own Cattlemen's Association of Crossbreeds is the best way to declare and protect our own market prices."

When no other questions came to the floor, Jake said, "this terminates my presentation. I hope I've convinced you that this is the road to the future. Now, for that last surprise I promised you, WILL THE REAL EMMITT POWELL PLEASE STAND."

Silence fell on the group till a presumed rancher pushed his chair back, slowly stood up and said, "Yes, I'm Emmitt and I came here to sell purebred and crossbreed stock. I have enough animals that I can complement your herds with the 1:20 ratio and match that number with the appropriate heifers. I will sell all three breeds, Hereford, Durhams and Texas Crossbreeds. Black Angus will be available in one year. For those of you who wish to make a purchase, please join me at that table up front. I will take your bank voucher as full payment."

Ranchers responded like an erupting volcano,

as polite as possible, eighteen ranchers bumped their way into a line to meet with Powell. The Duo saw two ranchers with their wives and foreman talking in the back of the canopy. The Duo stepped up to them as one rancher said, "we both agree that this is the only sensible way to go. However, we used up all our funds to buy your hay to get our herds thru winter. So, we're going to wait a year to buy new breeding stock."

Jake forcefully said, "nonsense, just follow Hannah to the office, and she'll take care of this problem. I'll see you when you come back."

Hannah asked how many cattle they had ready to breed. They both had around 400 head. Hannah did the math and came up to needing twenty bulls and twenty heifers. To be sure, she rounded it to 25 of each bulls and heifers, and evenly distributed over the three breeds. She said, "25 bulls at $60 each is $1,500 and 25 heifers at $40 each is $1,000. Hannah hands each rancher a personal bank draft for $2,500. Both ranchers objected and said, "we can't afford this loan, we can't even pay the interest say nothing of yearly payments." Hannah adds, "gentlemen, this is not a loan or a gift, it is a business advancement. There is no interest and there are no yearly payments. If you ever make a profit with this herd change, then you can pay it back over years per the original principal. This money comes from our Benefactor Fund and if you ever pay it back, the money will go back in the Benefactor Fund to help others in need. Now, go back in line and order what you need. This is our pleasure. but please keep this confidential to protect the Benefactor Fund."

When the two ranchers returned, Jake heard a discussion at Powell's table. "Ok, you need 30 bulls and heifers. Computing the cost, the rancher looked at the figures and said, "that comes to $3,000. Well I'll take half the order since $1,500 is all I have to spare." Powell knew what Jake had planned. He took a paper and wrote on it $1,500/$3,000 and signed the paper. He then said, "go to the office across the yard and see Mrs. Harrison. She'll solve this problem. The man got up and stared at the paper. Jake stepped up, looked at the paper and smiled. "Hannah will take care of this sir, please step off to the office."

By the end of the day, Emmitt Powell had sold all the stock he had hoped to. The Cattlemen's Association would be established, and the Crossbreed herd would become an entity.

***

In November, Jake busied himself with making changes. He had Cass Construction extend the baling platform to allow three more baling sites for future use. He also had a carriage shed added to the barn to hold buggies, buckboards, basic wagons, and hay wagons. He also built a separate blacksmith shop and moved Washington from the barn addition to his own shop, with ample room to bring in implements and wagons for repairs. Anticipating the purchase of phosphate fertilizer in the future, he built a storage shed with three-foot concrete walls to hold the phosphate bags or bulk. The last change was to expand the barn to hold the remuda during winter months.

As the holidays approached, Hannah finally went into labor. She spent five hours in moderate labor and only a short time in hard labor. Erna and Camilla spent every minute with her and were there for the delivery. Jake and Amos spent anxious hours worrying about a natural process that they had no control over and weren't even allowed to participate in. Doc Craven came to the waiting room frequently to reassure the 'useless' men that everything was going well. No one knew that outside the hospital doors was a quiet conclave of their workers, friends, businessmen men, neighbors and well-wishers who just wanted to hear that everything was OK or hear the cry of a baby.

When Jake and Amos heard the cry of a baby, they both knew that a miracle had just happened. When Jake was invited in Hannah's room he froze. He saw his beautiful wife holding their child in a blue blanket. Hannah said, "Jake, it's time for you to meet and hold your healthy son. Years later Erna said that Jake was frozen in time with a perpetual smile on his face and a tear trying to leave the corner of his eye. It took him at least fifteen minutes to thaw out so he could hold his son.

That winter, Jake spent most of his time with Hannah and their baby. By April, Jason was crawling all over the house. He was a happy baby that always had a smile and rarely cried. Even with Hannah nursing the baby, she was again with child within a month of resuming relations. Hannah was proud as could be. It was a pleasure to raise her son and her husband had become more attached to the family than had been anticipated.

Meanwhile, Clayton had been busy supplementing the herd with hay fed in hay bins to minimize wastage. Fortunately, the winter had only traces of snow with temperatures in the forty degrees. The cattle could still eat the winter dead grass and with the hay supplements did very well throughout the winter months.

By April, Jake and Hannah were sitting by the fireplace after Jason was down for the night. Jake said, "we've been so fortunate, and we've come a long way, babe. Spring is here, we have a healthy son, you're pregnant again, you just started your second book, your first book has sold out four printings and is now in mass production, our oil wells are each still holding at 100 barrels a day, our herd is doing well, we're at peace with our neighbors, and we have great people working for us."

Hannah interjected, "and we are both in our mid-twenties. We could easily spend the next 25 years on this homestead, enjoying our family, hobbies and businesses. But I know you, you'll find another business to add to this Harrison Empire."

Jake came back, "now you see what has come about since you agreed to marry me, and you even suspect that more is to come. So, when did you suspect, for the first time, that this could ever happen?"

"Mister Harrison, let me say this. When you rescued me from those would be rapist goons, I initially assumed that once the three animals were bound up, that you would rape me instead of them. But then, with me in full nudity, you calmly said to check the rapist's clothes for pants, shirt and boots that would fit me. Then you said the phrase that disrupted my brain. You said, 'please get dressed, Miss.' I knew at that moment that we would spend the rest of our lives together."

And that is how a young couple started their family, their homestead, their hobbies and their businesses in the early 1890's. This was their true destiny, heh?

***

The End